INSIDE THE MAZE

AND THE ANIMAL EXPERIMENTS
ALICE SAW THERE

Mark Jerram

Jacob's Old Shoes

First published 1996
by Jacob's Old Shoes

Revised 1997

This paperback edition 2014

ISBN-13: 978 0953081318
ISBN-10: 0953081311

"Inside the Maze is humorous, informative and moving – a very worthwhile book."
Tony Page, Doctor of Philosophy in Literature.

"An excellent read and very thought provoking."
Lynsey Dye (Naturewatch).

"Mark has managed to get everything in – it is amazing."
Gill Redfearn (Plan 2000).

"A very novel approach to exposing vivisection."
Jill Russell, DCR.

"Cleverly based on Alice in Wonderland, and quite brilliantly introduces the 'unscientificness' and futility of vivisection."
Joy Palmer (Doctors and Lawyers for Responsible Medicine).

CONTENTS

CHAPTER 1

DOWN THE TUBE

Alice had just finished playing with her farm-yard, and was now sitting at her bedroom window. She sometimes sat there for ages just watching the world go by.

Alice had been playing with her farm-yard for quite a while, and today the story had been about a farmer and his wife who had over slept. The animals were at first confused, as they didn't know how to act on their own.

The animals got together in an old barn, and decided that, as they knew what jobs had to be done about the farm, they would get on and do them. It was agreed that the cows would collect the hens' eggs; the hens would shear the sheep; the sheep would milk the cows; and the old work-horse would pull the plough across the fields.

The pigs, at first, didn't like this idea; but when they realised that all they had to do was spend the day eating, they agreed.

When the farmer and his wife eventually did wake up, all that day's work had been done. The farmer and his wife were so pleased with what the animals had done, that they invited them all into the farmhouse and gave them tea. Alice always liked ending her stories with everyone getting together and eating.

So now Alice sat at her window, and as the street was deserted she soon started day-dreaming. Her ornamental Noah's ark was on the windowsill beside her, and Alice started thinking about what would have happened if Noah and his family had over slept and missed getting aboard the ark.

Alice came out of her day-dream when she saw something move in the street below. It was her next-door neighbour with his dog, and just at that precise moment of her looking down, she saw the man kick his dog. It was not a tap, but a firm hard boot into the dog's side. Alice gasped and rose to her feet in alarm. She then looked around her bedroom to see where Mary, her dog, was, and to make sure she hadn't seen what had just happened. Mary had been lying fast asleep under the chair Alice had been sitting on, but now looked up at Alice because she had made a noise and risen so suddenly.

Alice patted Mary so to reassure her, then looked out of the window again. The man's dog was cowering and looking up at him. The man yanked the lead to make the dog start walking again.

They both disappeared round the corner. Alice stood there awhile, then went downstairs to tell her father what she had just seen.

"Dad, I've just seen our neighbour kick his dog," said Alice, rushing into the living-room.

"Yes?" her father replied, not looking up from the newspaper he was reading.

"Why did he do that?" Alice asked.

"I don't know."

"It must've hurt the dog."

"Well, I guess that was his intention."

"Oh! But that's just cruel," cried Alice.

"The world's a cruel place, Alice," said her father, finally taking a glimpse over the top of his paper. "As you will gradually find out more and more."

"I'm going to go and ask him why he did it."

"Don't be daft, Alice;" her father said rather sternly; "it hasn't got anything to do with you."

"But I think it has."

"Look, it's getting late," said her father; "I think it's time you were in bed. Anyway, it's a special day tomorrow, so the sooner you go to sleep the sooner it will be here. Come over here and give your old dad a good-night kiss."

"I shan't be able to sleep," complained Alice; "I want to know what made him do it."

"Perhaps the dog had been naughty," suggested her father.

"But you never smack me when I'm naughty," said Alice.

"Animals are different, Alice; you can't reason with an animal. You have to show them who's boss."

"Perhaps. But kicking as hard as he did can't be right."

Alice looked at her father and sensed that he was getting tired of the subject. "Oh why isn't he interested in it," thought Alice, "it's more important than his snooze-paper."

Alice went over to him, and hugged and kissed him good-night.

"Why are people cruel when love is so much better?" she said softly in her father's ear.

"I don't know Alice, but they do say that it's love that makes the world go round."

"Yes, that's a good thought," said Alice, more cheerfully, "that shall help me go to sleep tonight. Good-night dad."

"Good-night Alice, sweet dreams."

Alice went upstairs and got ready for bed. She kissed good-night each and every one of her soft toy-animals and then Mary.

"I could never kick you," Alice said to Mary.

She selected two of her soft toys and took them to bed with her. Alice was always very careful of avoiding any favouritism by making sure all her toy-animals got one turn in the period of a week. Alice wasn't allowed to have Mary in her bed. She had explained this to Mary, but Alice was quite certain Mary got jealous all the same.

Alice lay there, unable to get asleep. She tossed and turned as she kept on thinking about the poor dog.

"I bet that man is always cruel to that dog. I used to think he was nice. Well, he has always been friendly to me; he's even stroked Mary once. Well, I'm not going to let him do that again, and if he asks why, I will tell him. Dad can't tell me off for that, because I will be answering the man's question.

"Oh dear, this isn't helping me get to sleep at all. I need something to take my mind off it. I know, I'll put on a video."

Alice got out of bed and put on one of her videos. She knew she was too old for the one she had chosen, but liked the bit where it went through the windows and showed real life things.

Alice got back into bed and cuddled up with her toys. She fast-forwarded past the boring bits to just before the 'through the windows' section.

The woman on the video said, "Which window do you think it will be today? Let's see, as we go through the..." She paused, and the TV camera drew nearer the three windows. Alice quickly said aloud, "Round-window!" She always picked the Round-window as it was her favourite: she thought a round window a weird and futuristic shape for a house to have. But it was strange her picking it then, as she had seen the video many times before and knew exactly which window they would be going through. This was most probably why Alice was not too upset when the woman concluded with: "...through the Arch-window."

Now that the Arch-window had been chosen, it

moved closer and closer to the screen and then started to clear so to reveal the scene. But then, all of a sudden, the picture went fuzzy and started flashing.

"Oh dear, my video's got screwed up in the machine!" cried Alice.

Now, what with the room being dark and the television screen flashing, Alice soon started to feel quite funny. She wanted to get up and turn it off, but she was unable to. It was as if she had become a statue; her eyelids were stuck open and her eyes couldn't look away from the screen.

Finally, the screen stopped flashing and a normal picture resumed.

"This isn't what it's supposed to be," Alice thought to herself, when she saw what was now on the television screen. "It's meant to be about the life of a milk-bottle." But no matter how much she tried, she was still unable to move: only watch.

* * *

After some time the picture went fuzzy again, making Alice suddenly realise how sleepy she felt. Alice knew she would have to turn the television off before she went to sleep, but she was still unable to move.

"If I concentrate on moving just one small part of myself," Alice thought to herself, "and succeed in making that part move, the rest of my body might follow."

Alice nominated her tongue, and started trying to push it between her front teeth.

"It's as if my tongue weighs a ton," thought Alice, as her tongue was in no fit state to be used for anything like speaking.

Then all of sudden out it popped, and it was just as Alice had guessed, because as soon as that happened the rest of her body was released from its hold.

"What a peculiar way to break the spell," said Alice out loud, so to make full use of her now active tongue.

Alice got out of bed and went over to the television. Just as she was about to turn the television off she noticed that the fuzzy picture had gone, and in its place was the Arch-window. It filled up the whole screen and looked real. Alice put out her hand to touch it, and as her fingers felt the glass the Arch-window swung inwards. Alice looked inside but couldn't see anything.

"Oh how exciting!" cried Alice. "I bet the place in there is full of strange and wonderful things." She poked her head inside again. "I'll be able to go and have my very own adventures. I've got to climb inside. Oh what great adventures I'm bound to have. Yes, it'll be 'Alice Through The Arch-window (And What A Wonderful Time She Had There!)'

"But if this *is* a place full of strange and wonderful things, I'd better take my camera, because nobody believes the tales of children. My camera will be my proof."

Alice stepped into the dark place and immediately felt a chill run over her body. Ignoring this, Alice surveyed her surroundings and noticed she was in a dark tube that went far into the distance. "I wonder what's at the other end?" – no sooner had she thought this than she was off to find out.

Alice had only walked a small distance when she decided to turn round and see what her bedroom looked like from inside the television.

"I've spent many hours sitting out there looking at the TV," thought Alice, "and never once thought about it looking at me. It must get ever so bored, because I just sit there doing nothing. I'll have to start doing things while I'm watching the telly, it's only fair."

But what she saw wasn't her bedroom.

"Oh, what a beautiful garden!" cried Alice in surprise. "It's so bright and colourful, I can almost smell those flowers; and my animals are really enjoying themselves. But I wonder where my bedroom has got to?"

After looking upon such a beautiful garden, the dark tube seemed quite undesirable to Alice now. It was no longer the exciting curiosity it had once been.

"I think I'll return now; this place is dark, cold and I bet it's even haunted," said Alice, as she began making her way back. She could hear birds singing, some children playing and her dog barking with joy. She was so excited she forgot to look where she was going and banged her nose against something hard. It wouldn't have made much difference if she had been looking because she had run headlong into the transparent television screen.

"It's set fast! Not like it was before," cried Alice, as she tried desperately to open the television screen (as indeed that was what it was, as it no longer resembled anything like an arch-window).

Alice stood behind the glass and just watched them. They were playing, dancing, singing, laughing; in fact, they were acting just as if they were playing 'let's pretend' with Alice. They all seemed so happy; and seeing them made Alice also feel happy. It made her remember a song she had learned for her dancing class. Alice began singing it:

"Cats and Rabbits,
Would reside in funny little houses,
And be dressed in shoes and hats and trousers,
In a world—"

Alice was interrupted in her singing by a voice coming from somewhere behind her:

"Oh dear! Oh dear! How you do delay."

"I wonder who said that?" thought Alice, as she turned round but saw no-one there. "Ghosts! Oh dear, there *are* ghosts in here." Alice pressed her face and hands up against the screen.

"Alice," called the desperate sounding voice. But Alice made no acknowledgement of it.

"Alice," pleaded the now trembling voice.

"I suppose I should go and investigate," thought Alice. "Whoever it is sounds very in need."

So Alice walked in the direction of the voice. It was the only way she could go anyway: down the long dark tube. As Alice walked along she felt more and more uneasy, but kept on walking nevertheless. Every so often, Alice looked over her shoulder to see the light of the garden; it made her feel safer to think that her friends were there.

After walking for some time (exactly how long, Alice couldn't begin to guess) she again looked over her shoulder; but the light from the garden had finally disappeared into the darkness.

Alice paused, then said out loud, "I'm coming, Sir," trying to break the silence and reassure herself. Alice continued, and noticed that even the sound of her footsteps seemed to be swallowed up by the blackness.

"You need to get to the 5th floor," said the voice again.

"The 5th floor! And how am I to do that?" questioned Alice to herself; whereupon, she noticed a lift, faintly illuminated, directly in front of her.

"How did I miss that?" wondered Alice, as she pushed the button to call the lift. The doors opened and Alice was flooded in light. She shielded her eyes and stepped in.

"Oh dear, this lift only goes as far as the 4th," said Alice, once her eyes had accustomed themselves to the light. "So how am I to get to the 5th? I suppose I should go at least as far as the 4th."

Up went the lift, and Alice got out at the 4th floor. She tried each of the doors she came across, but they just opened onto empty rooms. Alice then looked at a small insignificant door that she had at first ignored because she had taken it to be nothing more than a broom cupboard or something.

"I suppose this is my last option," said Alice, without much hope. She opened the door, and there inside was a spiral staircase going upwards.

"This must lead to the 5th floor," said Alice, as she started to ascend the stairs. It gradually became darker and darker, until her surroundings were as black as when she had been in the tube.

Alice finally reached the top and stepped from the staircase. Owing to the darkness, Alice had to feel along the walls for a door. After a little searching she did find a door, but it was locked. She moved away so to feel for another door, when suddenly she fell through a hole in the floor and started sliding down something.

"Perhaps this is the snake to take me right back down to the bottom!" Alice exclaimed, once her stomach had receded from her mouth. But it wasn't just taking her down: she was sliding horizontally, and she even felt that sometimes she was sliding upwards! In the blackness she couldn't see which way she was going. She got so disorientated that she didn't know if she was going up, down, or inside out.

Suddenly, she fell out of the darkness and into a brilliant white room.

CHAPTER 2

THE WHITE ROOM

The first thing Alice saw was a rabbit. "I bet he was the one who called me here," she said, "or was it him, or him. Oh dear, there are so many!" There were rows upon rows of white rabbits in white boxes.

The walls, floor and ceiling were all painted white, and even the people were dressed in white. "Oh this is just as bad as the black place," said Alice.

"Who said that?" asked a white rabbit.

"I did," replied Alice.

"Could you kindly step onto my other side," said the White Rabbit, "so I can see you with my good eye."

Alice did as she was asked, then said, "I think you should wear a monocle for your bad eye, then you would be able to see on both sides."

The Rabbit looked startled by this idea; so, hoping to reassure him, Alice added:

"Really Sir, it's not as silly as it may sound, and they can make you look quite gentlemanly."

"I will if you insist," replied the Rabbit, "but I would prefer it if you left that eye alone for a little bit longer, please Miss."

"Don't worry, I won't touch your eye if you don't want me to," said Alice softly, "but honestly, Sir, I didn't intend doing anything of the sort."

"No?" said the White Rabbit quite surprised.

"What a sweet, dear rabbit he is," thought Alice, "very silly as well though. Fancy him thinking I wanted to touch his eye. I'm quite certain I never mentioned that I would." The White Rabbit looked so forlorn that Alice quite regretted ever mentioning the monocle.

It wasn't until this point that Alice looked at the White Rabbit's bad eye, and it was indeed bad. It was all swollen and seeping, and the rim of it looked extremely sore.

"I don't think a monocle could help that eye," thought Alice; "I was the one being silly for mentioning such a thing." Alice decided it was perhaps best to leave the subject of his eye alone, as he was obviously distressed about it and she had just made him feel worse. So Alice changed the subject:

"Was it you that called me, when I was in that dark tube?"

"Yes – when – no – I don't think – you won't tell anyone will you?" the White Rabbit said all in a fluster.

"You are such a nervous creature," said Alice, "why *should* I tell anyone? And anyway, what's so wrong with you calling out to me?"

"Oh I don't know," replied the Rabbit. "I don't know what's right or what's wrong down here. I just don't want to upset anyone."

"You should be the one upset," said Alice, "locked up in that box."

"And I am, but who cares if I'm upset, of course I get upset, I get upset all the time," said the Rabbit, as if he was about to cry any moment. "I would give anything to be out in the open fields right now; to feel the midday sun; to breathe in the crisp dawn air. Oh, how I would love to be out there – how I would love being a rabbit. But, alas! it's not to be, because I am locked up in this box. But that's neither here nor there – as I am here and you are there."

Alice felt she had said the wrong thing again, but what confused her most was the way the Rabbit had made her feel responsible.

"I think it's time you went now," said the Rabbit

despondently; "you also could get into trouble for talking to me."

"Aren't I allowed to be here?" questioned Alice.

"Of course you're not," said the Rabbit more assertively, as now he was concerned for Alice, who seemed to him very naive. "Oh dear. Do be careful."

So Alice stepped away from the White Rabbit. She looked down the line at all the other white rabbits. They all looked just as worried and sad as the one she had spoken to, and they all had that one bad eye. Alice couldn't bring herself to talk to any more of them. She just wanted to get out of that clinically white room, in which the only colours she could see were the rabbits' small and normal, pink eyes, alongside their hideous red, yellow, and purple eyes.

Alice looked around and noticed there was a large double-door along the wall in front of her, and three single doors on the opposite wall behind her.

Turning to the White Rabbit, Alice asked, "Which way should I go?"

"I'm afraid the best you can do is to just follow your nose and catch your tail," replied the Rabbit.

Alice went up to the large door and tried to open it, but it was bolted both top and bottom. After a struggle, Alice managed to slide back the bottom bolt; but there was no way she could reach the top bolt to even try to slide it open.

So Alice turned round and made for the other doors. One was red, one was blue, and the other was yellow. First she tried the red door but found it to be locked. Next she tried the blue door but that was also locked. The yellow door, at least, was different and opened for Alice when she pulled it.

Without hesitation, Alice walked through it, and as she did so, the White Rabbit said softly, "Dear innocent girl, forgive me."

CHAPTER 3

ROBOTS AND MONSTERS

Alice's eyes glanced around the new room she now found herself in. "Oh good, it's full of cats," said Alice to herself. Alice loved cats, and would have owned one if it weren't for her mother being allergic to them. This is not to say Alice didn't love her dog. For now that she had Mary she was glad her mother was allergic to cats, because Mary was quite possibly the best pet in the world.

Alice saw one of the cats continuously walking round in circles. "That's peculiar; I've never seen a cat do that before."

"Excuse me," Alice said to the cat; but it just continued walking around.

"Excuse me!" she said a bit louder; but the cat still ignored her. "Well I never, of all the rude things."

Alice soon gave up with this cat and looked around for a different one to talk to. Alice noticed one that was sitting still. "Perhaps he will be more talkative," thought Alice.

"Hello, I'm Alice. Your friend's ever so rude." The cat just sat there. "Perhaps all the animals in this room have got problems with their ears." And while Alice was thinking this, the cat's left pupil began to grow larger; then it started to shrink until it had nearly disappeared. It finally went back to its normal size.

"How odd!" thought Alice. Then the same thing happened to his right pupil. Alice was just about to talk to him again when he stuck out his tongue, gave a grimace, and then curled up his tongue and put it back into his mouth. "That happens to me when I taste lemons," thought Alice. "It was definitely as if he had tasted something bitter, but I know he hadn't. Well, at least I didn't see him lick or eat anything. Oh dear, his eyes are starting again now. This place is so strange."

Alice noticed another cat that first gave a sniff, then scratched his nose, only to repeat the procedure again. One cat, she felt sure was yawning. While another kept tapping his foot, as if he was listening to music.

"I know what it is, all these cats are robots," thought Alice. "Oh how wonderful!"

Alice felt better, now that she had worked out the reason for their peculiar ways.

"When they don't move they are so lifelike," thought Alice, "just like real cats. The only thing that lets their appearances down are those metal hats they're all wearing."

"Hello, I'm Alice," she said to the sniffing cat. "Haven't they taught any of you to talk yet?" The sniffing cat didn't answer, so Alice guessed that the answer must be no.

"Well, I can't have much of a conversation with any of you," said Alice. "I would've thought that, at least, they would have made you use a miaow to mean yes and a purr to mean no, so people could ask you simple questions."

"It must be so exciting making robots," thought Alice to herself, "bringing bits of metal and things to life." Then Alice happened to notice something about the cat's eyes. "Oh dear, his eyes are so sad. It seems as if he doesn't like sniffing and scratching all the time. I guess it can't be much fun being a robot. I'm sure I wouldn't like it."

The cat still looked at Alice. "I know you're sad, but we are what—" Alice cut herself short. She had intended to say 'we are what God made us' but realised God hadn't made him. This made Alice pity the cats even more.

Alice found it hard to look the cat in the eyes because they seemed so pleading: asking her to do something. What that something was, Alice had no idea.

Alice began to feel uneasy, so she looked around for a door to leave by; but the only ones in the room were the three coloured doors that would take her straight back into the room with the White Rabbit.

"Perhaps my journey has come to an end," thought Alice, "and I've got to return now."

Even though Alice expected the red and blue doors to be locked, she tried them all the same – and, yes, they were locked. Therefore, Alice had to use the same door she had entered by.

On stepping through, and to Alice's surprise, she didn't see the white rabbits, but a two-headed dog.

"Oh dear!" she cried.

"I know I look ugly, but you don't have to make your disgust so plainly obvious," said the larger of the two heads. "Do you think I enjoy having him joined to me?"

"Oh no, it wasn't that," said Alice full of remorse, "I wasn't expecting to find you in here. You weren't in here when I just left."

"We've been here all the time," said the smaller head. Who then, twisting his neck round (the best he could manage), looked at the other head, and said, "I don't particularly enjoy being joined to you, you know."

The larger head began to growl at the smaller head, who in answer gave a vicious snarl, followed by a bark. They both bared their teeth and began snapping at each other.

"Oh do stop!" pleaded Alice. "Someone will get— er, you'll hurt yourself— yourselves." Alice couldn't work out the numbers involved in the fight, whether it was one, two, or perhaps even one and half!

"Why do you fight so?" asked Alice, once they had finally calmed down.

"Because he's being imposing," replied the larger head. "Do you know, he even eats my food."

"Well, you licked my paw the other day," said the smaller head angrily. "I call that being imposing."

"Does it matter who eats the food, when it so obviously goes to the same belly," interposed Alice, as she feared they might start fighting again. "And if he licks your paw, it's because he thinks it's his paw."

"I know what's mine, and he's always being imposing," they both said together. This caused them to glare at each other from the corners of their eyes, and resume their fight.

"Stop it! Do you hear me! Stop it this minute!" cried Alice, realising at once she was acting like her school teacher. The effect worked and they ceased fighting.

"You two are insufferable," said Alice, still partly in her school teacher role.

"Inseparable, you mean," said the larger head.

"How can you joke about it?" said the smaller head; and these words seemed to be the bell for round three.

Alice tried to break up the fight, but there was no coming between them this time. She decided perhaps it was best she left, and then they might calm down.

Alice looked around, and still she only had the choice of those same three doors.

"I bet that dog's tail never wags," thought Alice. "Those two heads couldn't agree on who the tail belonged to, so they would have a fight over it and then there'd be no need for the tail to wag anymore. Oh what a sad dog he must be. I'll never believe it again when people tell me that two heads are better than one."

Using the yellow door, Alice stepped out of the room.

CHAPTER 4

HEAR, SEE, AND SPEAK

The first thing Alice noticed on entering the next room was the noise. There was a constant clickerty-clack and buzzing. The noises were coming from a long line of monkeys who were working at machines. Each monkey was strapped into a chair and sat facing a panel that was covered with different lights and buttons. Whenever a light flashed on or a buzzer sounded the monkeys immediately pressed the button closest to it. Also, the monkeys were continually tapping their left feet on a pedal.

"I didn't know people got monkeys to work for them," said Alice to herself. "I suppose it's a good idea because monkeys *are* clever animals. It's a bit like the monkey's tea party I saw last year; oh that was funny, especially when they climbed onto the table and started chucking food around. Actually, this is quite funny as well – I don't know if it's meant to be; but animals always do look funny when they act like people."

All the while Alice was thinking this to herself, the monkeys diligently continued their work and didn't take the slightest notice of Alice.

"They are hard workers," thought Alice, "but I can't see what the work is going to produce."

Alice walked over to one of the monkeys. "Excuse me, Sir, can I talk to you?"

"No; I haven't got time," said the Monkey sternly. But Alice persisted, "Please, it'll only take a minute of your time."

"Only a minute!" cried the Monkey. "You brush it

off so lightly, as if it's nothing."

"Well, a minute isn't much, if you think about it," said Alice, "in fact, it's only sixty seconds."

"But it's also one sixtieth of an hour," said the Monkey, while still working ceaselessly. "Look after the minutes, and the hours will look after themselves."

"Why does a minute *need* looking after?" asked Alice.

"Because, before you know where you are, they've gone," explained the Monkey.

"I could've spoken to you by now, while we've been talking about wasting time," moaned Alice.

"See what I mean, they pass so easily," said the Monkey.

"Really, I don't think I'm asking for much – only a minute," said Alice, losing her patience.

"Well, a minute is something I haven't got!" snapped the Monkey. "Why, just giving you a minute could cost me dearly."

"There's no need for you to stop working," said Alice, coaxingly. "I'm sure you can work and talk at the same time. Then you'll be doing two things at once, and that's sure to save time."

"Yes, that's true," said the Monkey. "Okay, I will talk to you, and then perhaps with all the time I've saved, I will be able to fit in a few more taps on the pedal."

"What is it you're doing?" said Alice, getting straight into her first question.

"I press the buttons when I'm signalled to do so," explained the Monkey.

"Oh," said Alice. "And why do you tap your foot so much?"

"Well you see," said the Monkey, turning and looking at Alice for the first time, "when the feeding light is on I have to tap that pedal fifty consecutive times if I want to receive any food at the break-time. If I don't reach that quota I'll go hungry."

While the Monkey had been speaking, Alice had noticed that he had missed one of the lights. She was about to tell him, when suddenly the Monkey bared his teeth in a painful grimace and let out a chattering cry.

"What's the matter?! What's wrong?!" cried a concerned and flustered Alice.

"Blast you! See what you made me do," shouted the Monkey angrily, "you made me miss pressing the button."

"I am sorry," said Alice, "but was it really as serious as all that. I mean, you did cry out so; I thought something really bad was wrong with you."

The Monkey, who was once again concentrating on his panel, yelled back at Alice: "I was given an electric shock! As punishment!"

Alice didn't know what to say, and even if she had known, she would have kept quiet for fear of disturbing him. So Alice moved away from all the monkeys to let them work.

Suddenly, it went quiet; the lights and buzzers had all stopped and the monkeys were now able to rest.

"This must be their break and feed time," thought Alice.

The monkeys that had reached the specified quota of taps now received their food. Down a shoot and into a tray, at the side of the machines, fell a small pellet. These, the monkeys popped into their mouths, gave a couple of bites, then swallowed. The other unlucky monkeys kept checking their food trays, in the small hope of finding a pellet.

In a couple of minutes the monkeys were all busy back at work again.

Alice went into the next room, and what a stark contrast she found compared with the last room. Here, there was hardly any noise, just a low hum. The room was lined with square containers that had glass fronts. Alice walked along them and noticed that inside each of the containers was a cage and inside the cage was a monkey.

"This is just like a zoo," thought Alice; "why, at least they look like animals in a zoo."

Alice went up to one of the containers to have a closer look at the monkey inside. He became very excited at seeing Alice, and came up to the glass.

. "Hello," said Alice.

The monkey was obviously chattering excitedly but Alice couldn't hear a sound. This was because the containers had an air-tight seal.

Alice opened the glass front, and straight away the monkey put out his hand to touch her. Alice held his hand, which seemed to please him very much, but she could still sense his sadness.

"It must be these bars," thought Alice, as she tried opening the cage door. "I'm sorry, but they're locked," she said aloud.

"I know they are," said the Monkey, "but it's just good to feel you, and to hear another voice apart from my own. Normally, I can only look at that monkey directly opposite me."

"I think I should go and see some of the others," said Alice, "I'll leave your glass door open while I do."

"If you're going to open up any other containers," said the Monkey, "I'll ask you to close my door."

"Why's that?" asked Alice.

"Well, I don't want to get what they've got," said the Monkey.

"What do you mean?" asked Alice.

"See those big red crosses on their glass fronts,"

began the Monkey, "well, that means they've been injected with some contagious disease."

"Did you say, injected or infected?" queered Alice.

"Injected," clarified the Monkey.

"What, on purpose?" asked Alice.

"Of course," said the Monkey.

"Oh, how horrible!" cried Alice.

She then slowly made her way to one of the cages. Inside, she saw a monkey swaying backwards and forwards and muttering to himself; he made no acknowledgement of Alice being there.

"He's gone completely mad, you know," said the Monkey. "Isolation does that to you. They put you in here from the time you're born, until the time you die. I haven't been in here long; but he's been locked away, isolated from any contact, for about twenty years."

Alice went to the next one, who obviously wasn't mad, as his face manifested such clear unhappiness. He looked at Alice then put his hand through the bars and placed the palm of it flat against the glass door. Alice did the same on her side of the glass, directly opposite his hand.

"I think it might be best to go mad here," surmised Alice, as she looked into the monkey's face. "I had never realised before, just how *human* monkeys are."

"You don't know what you're talking about," rebuked the Monkey angrily.

"I do," said Alice, turning round to face him. "I know that Man descended from Apes."

"If it had to be any way, then sure, that would've been the way," said the Monkey, "but it is a lie; we are very different. I think you should leave now."

"Sure," said Alice; "but I'm sorry if—"

"And can you shut my glass front," interrupted the Monkey.

Alice did what she was instructed to do.

"It does seem wrong, him ordering me around so," thought Alice, as she entered the next room, "and for me to follow his orders, but these animals are so easily upset I think it was for the best."

This next room contained just one large cage; in which, cowering in a far corner, was a baby monkey.

"Are you all right?" asked Alice, as she could see it was definitely scared of something.

"Go away, leave me alone," pleaded the Baby Monkey.

"I can't leave you like this, when there's obviously something troubling you," insisted Alice. "If you tell me what it is, perhaps I can help."

"I don't want help," the Baby Monkey said softly, "I just want to die."

Alice was totally shocked by this. She couldn't understand how any living creature could wish to be dead. "Why do you want to die?" she asked.

"Because I don't want to live," said the Baby Monkey.

"*Yes*," said Alice, "but *why* don't you want to live?"

"Because to live is evil, evil and horrible – and scary." Here the Baby Monkey started to cry.

Alice wished she could go into the cage and cuddle him. She tried the door but it was shut tight. As it was impossible for her to cuddle him, Alice decided to try to reassure him with words:

"I know there's evil in the world, but there's a lot of love too."

"What do you know," was the Baby Monkey's sharp reply.

"Well, my dad told me that it is love that makes the world go round," said Alice, feeling quite offended by his last remark.

"That might be the way in your world," returned the Baby Monkey, "but for this world it's people minding their own business that causes it to keep turning. So you see, there are two possible options for me, but I know that the only realistic chance is for me to die."

Alice had no answer for this. She wasn't even sure what he had meant.

"Oh dear, I believe I've upset another one of these animals," thought Alice. "I wish I knew what was going on here; it all seems so very strange. Why can't someone explain it to me, then perhaps I could be of some help." She looked deploringly at the Baby Monkey, "All the animals I have met here have been such sad creatures."

Alice turned round, and as she made for the yellow door, said aloud, "There has to be an answer to this."

The Baby Monkey raised his head and said, in a voice not much louder than a whisper, "Death is my answer."

"No!" cried Alice, as she stepped out of the room, "there has to be a better way."

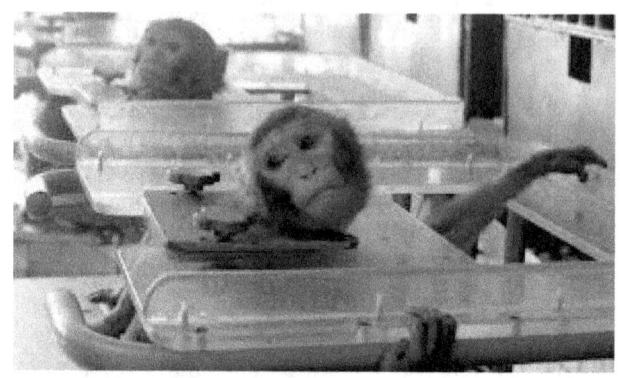

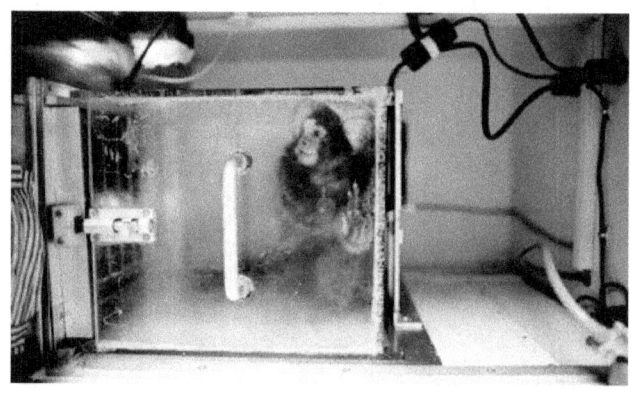

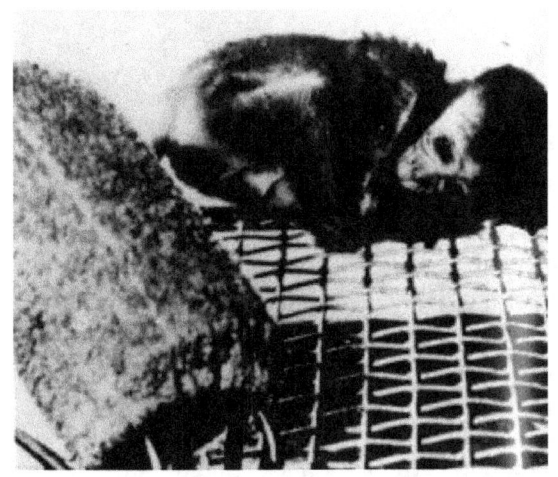

CHAPTER 5

SIN AND SORROW

Before Alice entered the next room, she was a little startled at seeing a kitten up in the top corner of the door-frame. It was so small and fluffy it could have been one of her toy animals. A kitten couldn't be cuter: with its big blue eyes and such an endearing black mark on its pink nose. Alice immediately adored it. (It is the kitten pictured at the front of this book.) And even though the corners of its little mouth did turn down slightly, it didn't look quite as sad as all the other animals she had seen so far. So Alice decided that perhaps it would be all right to ask it some questions, without having to worry whether she was upsetting it or not.

"Hello, can I help you?" said Alice first of all, thinking that the kitten might be stuck in the corner of the door.

"Oh no, you can't help me," said the Kitten.

On looking more closely, Alice couldn't see how it could be stuck, or even how it stayed up there, as it wasn't supported or holding on to anything. It just seemed to float.

"Do you understand what is happening here?" asked Alice.

"I know *what* is happening, but I can't say I fully understand," said the Kitten.

"Do you know that monkey in there?" said Alice, pointing behind her (despite the fact, the Baby Monkey and the room were no-longer there).

"I do," replied the Kitten.

"Can you think of any answer I could've given him that would've been better than his own answer?" asked Alice.

"He gave you that answer as well," said the Kitten.

"He did?" said Alice slightly confused; "well, what was it then?"

"Keep asking questions," was all the Kitten replied.

Alice was truly confused now. "What sort of answer is that?" she thought; but decided to follow his instruction: "Why was that monkey so sad?"

"Oh, he can't help that," said the Kitten, "we're all sad here. I'm sad. You're sad."

"How do you know I'm sad?" said Alice.

"You must be," said the Kitten, "but if you're not, then you must belong to the other lot – and be mad."

"I don't think I'm mad either," said Alice.

"Then what are you doing here?" said the Kitten; "all that are here are either sad or mad."

"I'm not sure," said Alice; "I suppose it was curiosity that brought me here."

"Why, that proves it then," said the Kitten, "you're definitely one of the mad kind. You're all extremely curious."

"But aren't you ever curious?" asked Alice.

"It killed the cat, you know," remarked the Kitten.

"But it doesn't always have to mean that," said Alice.

"Here, that is always the result," said the Kitten.

"Why don't all the sad animals leave here?" enquired Alice.

"Are you going to take them?" asked the Kitten.

"I don't know if I should," was all Alice could think of as a reply.

The Kitten then vanished, leaving that last question in Alice's head: 'Are you going to take them?' She knew she hadn't answered it properly, but why was it down to her to take them.

"Oh, why has he gone? There were so many questions I wanted to ask him," said Alice to herself.

Alice stood there in the doorway; she didn't want to go into the next room. She waited absolutely still, hoping the Kitten would reappear. Alice knew that if she stepped just one inch forward she would be in the next room.

"I wonder what is in there. It's strange that I can't see inside. If I *was* able to see in there, then I could decide whether or not to go in. Well, I'm not going in there – I feel it's full of unpleasant things."

Alice's patience was rewarded when the Kitten reappeared.

"Are you waiting for me?" asked the Kitten. "I thought we had finished."

"It's rude to disappear like that," said Alice. "You didn't even say goodbye."

"Oh, I do apologise," said the Kitten sarcastically.

"And I need to know what's in the next room," insisted Alice.

"In the next room you will encounter some more results of vivisection," the Kitten informed her.

Alice liked learning new long words and hearing the sounds they made. She repeated this word to herself, "Viv-vee-sek-tion," breaking it down into its component parts.

"Vivisection sounds a horrible word," decided Alice.

"Yes," was all the Kitten said, before once again disappearing.

"He didn't really explain what was in there, and I still feel uneasy about it," said Alice to herself. "I know, I'll go back the way I came and return home. This is no place for a girl, anyway."

Alice tried to turn round so she could retrace her steps, but she was unable to.

"This is so unfair, I can either go into the next room

or else stay here for the rest of my life," said poor Alice despairingly.

Alice was actually contemplating her dilemma for a few moments, until she decided to try to think of a better solution. She soon came up with an idea:

"I know what I'll do, I'll quickly step in, and then pop back out again straight away. Then forwards will be what is now backwards and behind me will be the vivi-whatsit room, which I won't be able to go into because it will then be behind me. Oh, I do think I can be very clever sometimes."

(It was indeed a clever plan, but even the best plans can't be expected to see unforeseen problems.)

So Alice moved an inch forward and found herself in the next room. But once in the room, she found she couldn't just turn round and leave straight away, because she was transfixed. Alice wanted to leave more than anything in the whole world, but she couldn't. What she now looked upon were the worst things she had ever seen. Alice's eyes stared ahead, absorbing everything at once, and examining each one individually. The horrors she saw were such a shock to her that she couldn't move, scream or cry – even though she dearly wanted to.

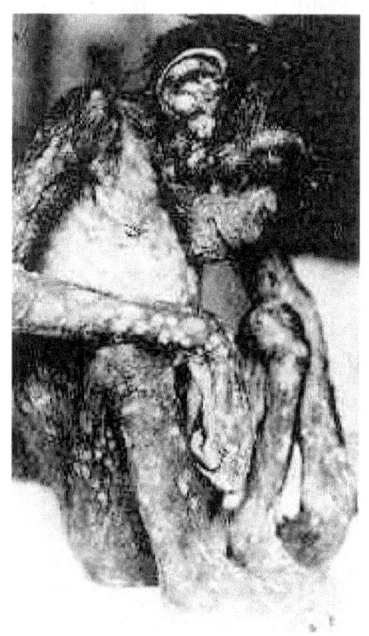

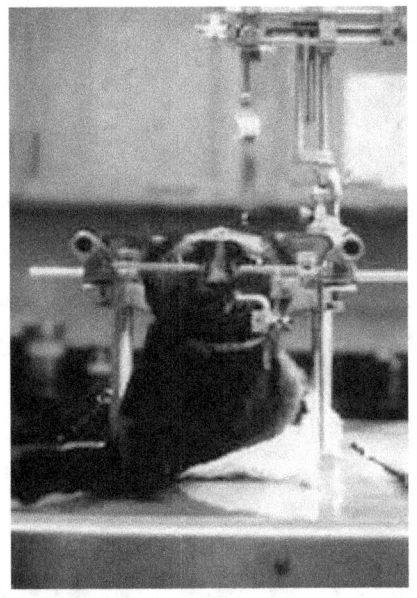

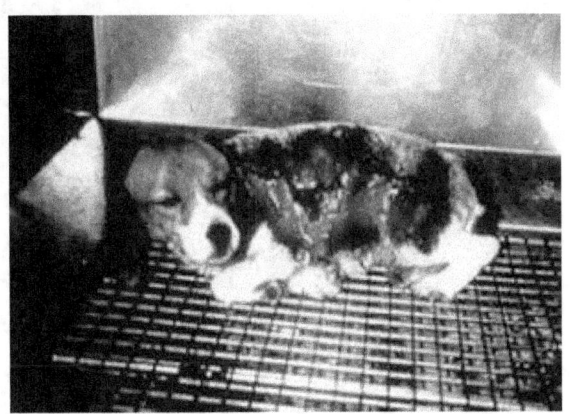

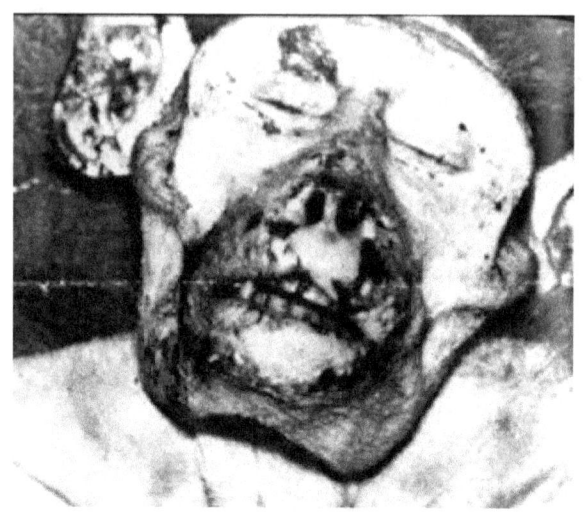

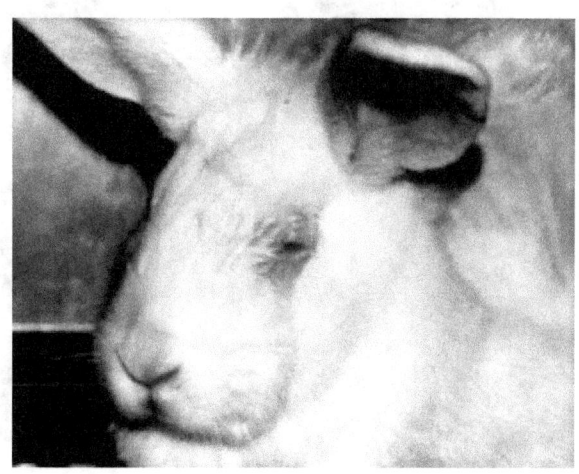

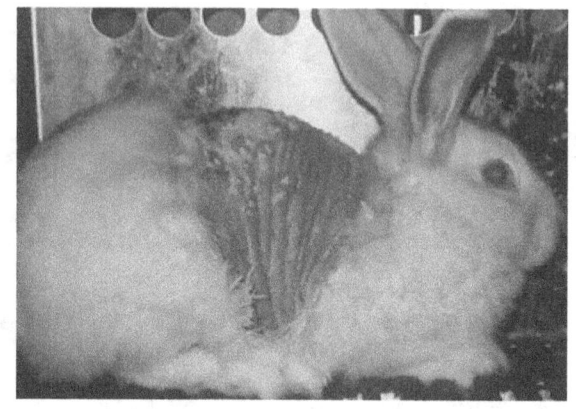

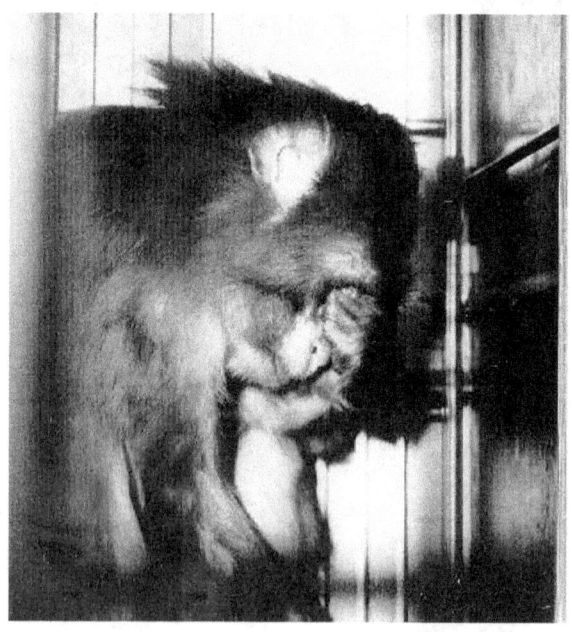

Alice stood absolutely still; only her eyes moved, looking from one animal to the next; each one adding to her disbelief. The mutilations she saw stung her eyes – the faces tore at her heart.

"Why!?" Alice was finally able to scream. She turned round and ran back into the doorway.

"That was surely hell," thought Alice, "that can be the only explanation."

Alice looked up and saw that the Kitten had returned. She had so much to ask him, so much she needed explained, but she couldn't think of a single question.

The Kitten looked at Alice and knew how confused she was – how frightened she was. He had meant to tell Alice everything when she returned from the room. He had to tell somebody; people had to know. But now he had doubts: was he telling the wrong person, did he have a right to tell her. But *he* had been made to experience sin and sorrow – and she had seen so much already. Yes, he would tell her. But where should he start – how should he start. He knew he couldn't tell everything – explain everything. But he knew he had to start.

"What you just saw," began the Kitten hesitantly, "were the results of vivisection. Vivisection is when people do experiments on animals to see how it affects them. These experiments cause the animals pain, distress, and end with the animals' death."

"So all the animals I've seen today," said Alice, "were being used in this way." The Kitten gave a nod. "No wonder they are all so sad."

"The rabbits were being used to test normal household products, like washing up liquid, lighter fuel, bleach, deodorant, anything and everything. They were testing to see how these products affected their eyes. They will keep on applying the product until the eye is affected, even if it means applying huge quantities.

"They use white rabbits because they are more

susceptible: the skin over their eyes is ten times thinner than a person's; and also, rabbits haven't any water ducts in their eyes, so they are unable to wash any of the product away."

Alice thought how sad the rabbits must be and that they couldn't even cry. A tear appeared in her eye. She wiped it away guiltily. "What is the point of these tests?" she asked.

"To see if the products might cause damage to the eyes of people," said the Kitten.

"Those cats you thought were robots," continued the Kitten, "aren't robots but real cats. Those metal hats are interfaces that have been inserted into their brains and then connected to a machine. A person at a keyboard makes them do all those things you saw them do. The cats have no control over their own bodies.

"That two-headed dog had started out life as two separate dogs, but somebody thought it would be a good idea to cut off the head from one dog and join it to another dog. With the animal being in pain and the heads undoubtedly confused about the situation, they just keep attacking each other.

"Those working monkeys are being trained to do certain tasks. They are taught to press buttons when a light or buzzer indicates to do so. They learn by punishment: if they don't press a button they receive an electric shock. Once they are trained and can perform the job well they are then exposed to radiation. From doing this, the experimenters can see what levels of radiation affect the monkeys ability to perform the tasks correctly.

"That cowering baby monkey you asked about before is in a test that is trying to induce depression. First the baby monkey was taken away from its mother as soon as it was born, and placed in a cage on its own, where it received no contact with any animal or human. (This, in fact, is a whole field of research in its self, where the baby monkeys suffer maternal and social deprivation.) But in this experiment they took it a step further. They wanted to look at attachment, and to see if it could be broken. You see, a baby monkey needs to make an attachment with its mother or another monkey, just like human babies do. But that opportunity was taken away from it. So when the experimenters gave the baby monkey a cloth surrogate mother to cling to, the baby monkey accepted it as its real mother and became attached to it. The experimenters then devised it so the cloth mother would turn into different monsters, hence trying to break that attachment. I will read to you what the experimenters themselves wrote about their tests:

> *The first of these monsters was a cloth monkey mother who, upon schedule or demand, would eject high-pressure compressed air. It would blow the animal's skin practically off its body. What did the baby monkey do? It simply clung tighter and tighter to the mother, because a frightened infant clings to its mother at all costs. We did not achieve any psychopathology. However, we did not give up. We built another surrogate monster mother that would rock so violently that the baby's head and teeth would rattle. All the baby did was cling tighter and tighter to the surrogate. The third monster we built had an embedded wire frame within its body which would spring forward and eject the infant from its ventral surface. The infant would subsequently pick itself off the floor, wait for the frame to return into the cloth body, and then cling again to the surrogate. Finally, we built our porcupine mother. On command, this mother would eject sharp brass spikes over all of the*

ventral surface of its body. Although the infants were distressed by these pointed rebuffs, they simply waited until the spikes receded and then returned and clung to the mother."

Alice stood there quietly, wondering what the point of it all was, and how it could be allowed to happen. She looked up and saw the Kitten just before he disappeared.

CHAPTER 6

ALICE WAKES UP

Alice lay there with her eyes shut. "No, it couldn't have been," she thought. "Perhaps it was. Well, I won't know for sure until I open my eyes."

Alice slowly opened her eyes. "Yes!" she shouted when she saw that she was in her bed. "So it was all just a very bad dream," said a relieved Alice. "I am so pleased."

She lay there thinking about her dream. "How could I dream such horrible things, things that scared me, and I really don't know how I remained asleep through it all. Oh, I am so glad it wasn't real though." Alice took a deep breath and then released it slowly. "It is so lovely to wake up after a bad dream and then realise that was all it was, just a dream, not real at all, it didn't happen, you can forget it, and everything is just the same as it was before you went to sleep."

Alice looked about her bed for one of her toy animals to cuddle, but she was unable to find any. She decided to look on the floor in case they had fallen there during the night. On doing so, Alice noticed that the floor was different, it wasn't her carpet. She looked round her bedroom and saw that the walls weren't pink as they should have been – but white!

Alice's heart dropped: sank to an unfathomable depth. She now realised that it wasn't her bedroom but another of those white rooms. One of those *real* white rooms.

Alice got out of bed, walked towards the yellow door, and passed through it.

Alice had been expecting to carry on from where she had left off, and to see more cases of animal experiments. So it was a nice surprise for Alice, when the room she entered next was practically empty. All that was in there was a man, dressed in a white coat, standing a little way in front of her.

"Oh, good!" said the Man, when he noticed Alice. "Now I'll be able to have a proper competitive game. I take it, you do want to play a game of Snakes and Ladders?"

"I don't mind," said Alice.

"Good-o," said the Man. "Right, let's start then."

"But where's the board?" enquired Alice.

"You're standing on it," said the Man. "It's a life-sized one. It covers the whole floor."

Alice looked down to where she was standing, and indeed she was standing on a square that had the number 1 written on it. She looked up and saw that the Man was standing on square 3. The rest of the board stretched out across the whole floor, right up to the walls. Large snakes and ladders had been painted on it just like a proper Snakes and Ladders board. And of course, the longest snake had its head placed in the last square but one, and slithered right back to square 8, the nearest any snake brought you back to the start.

"This could be fun," thought Alice. She then looked up at the Man, and, with great expectancy, asked, "How big is the dice?"

"Oh we don't use a dice, we use a coin," said the Man. "When it's your turn you toss the coin, and if it's heads you go one square forward, and if it's tails you go one square back."

"Are you going to come back and start at square one?" asked Alice.

"No, why should I? It ain't my fault you arrived late, now is it?" replied the Man. "I will let you go first, if you want. Now, I can't be fairer than that, can I."

Alice tossed the coin, and it was heads, so she stepped onto square 2.

The Man did the same, and also got heads, so stepped onto square 4, which had the first ladder placed in it. He raced along the ladder, singing: "You can't catch me, I'm the Gingerbread Man." He now stood on square 18.

Alice flipped her coin, and it was tails. She sighed and stepped back to square 1.

The Gingerbread Man got heads again, and moved another square forward.

Alice flicked her coin high into the air, and let it fall to the floor. It spun for a bit, then finally settled on tails. Alice stepped backwards from square 1 and out of the room.

"What a stupid game that was," said Alice, as she walked through the doorway and into the next room.

This new room Alice entered was dark, so dark in fact that she was unable to see what it contained. She stood there wondering what to do. Slowly, as her eyes became used to the darkness, she began to make out small shapes moving about not very far from her. She could also hear scratching and squeaking noises. Alice became nervous; she turned round to leave; but then by the door she noticed a light switch. She turned it on, looked round and found herself standing in a room full of rats!

Suddenly, the air was filled with smoke and laughter. There were tables scattered about the room with rats seated round them playing cards. All the rats were puffing at cigarettes, drinking beer and eating Big-Fat burgers. The floor was strewn with rubbish: dog-ends, empty bottles, hypodermic needles, rotting food, and, of course, polystyrene boxes. All the rats seemed jovial, as they talked and laughed with each other.

At one table the pot-money was getting bigger and bigger. One by one the rats at this table dropped out until just two were left. Soon all the rats in the room were crowding around the table. Some were shouting support for the grey rat named Dick, and others were egging on the brown rat called Bill. As the money increased so did the smoking and drinking.

"I'll see ya," said Dick finally. By now there was a mountain of money on the table. The two rats were engulfed in bodies as the other rats pushed forward and climbed over each other to see the result. Bill put his cards on the table, and by the reaction of everyone Alice gathered it must have been a very good hand.

Just then, Dick shouted out in pain, placed his hand on his chest and slumped forward.

"Come on Dick, what ya got!" shouted one of the rats from the crowd. "Show us first, then ya can die to yer 'art's content." There was a ripple of laughter around the crowd.

Having recovered slightly, Dick sat up, took away his hand, and laid his cards on the table.

Bill looked at them and turned pale. He stood up and yelled, "You cheating dirty—"

"No way, mate," Dick quickly replied. "'Ow could I of cheated wiv so many watchin'."

"I'm not stupid you know!" shouted Bill. "You swapped the cards when you put yer hand on yer chest and slipped 'em under yer jacket."

Bill then smashed a bottle on the side of the table, rose quickly to his feet and pointed his weapon at Dick. In doing this, Bill had upset the table, causing the cards and money to be knocked up into the air. There was mayhem as rats fought to grab as much money as they could.

Dick, who was oblivious to the commotion, coolly took out a gun, and without hesitation shot Bill. And as Bill fell to the floor, Dick clutched his chest again.

"Are you all right?" a voice asked. Alice looked up and on seeing a big rat only inches from her face stepped back. The room, Alice now noticed, had calmed down and the rats were all safely in cages.

"Are you all right?" asked the rat again (who, incidentally, Alice thought looked just like Dick).

"Yes thank-you," answered Alice automatically. "Well, I think so. Just now, I saw all you rats smoking, drinking, fighting—"

"Well of course you did," interrupted Dick (I think we might as well call him that), "that's what we do here. Look," he pointed round the room.

"She doesn't care," snapped another rat, before Alice had had a chance to look round the room. Alice turned to this rat and saw Bill glaring at her.

"What do you mean 'I don't care'?" asked Alice.

"You don't like us, you don't care what happens to us," accused Bill. "We're vermin – sewer dwelling, diseased ridden, plague spreading vermin. R-r-rats-s-s." The way he rolled the R and drew out the S on the word 'rats' was intended to be both comical and frightening. And indeed, Alice trembled while Bill laughed.

Alice had to admit to herself that she wasn't very keen on rats, but the main thing she disliked about them was their tails. She looked towards Dick for support.

"You'll just have to ignore him," he said. "It's the experiment they're doing on him that makes him act like that. You see, they're testing the link between alcohol and aggression."

"Well, he is definitely aggressive," said Alice.

"Yes, and paranoid, and argumentative, but I'm sure people already know that. I'm quite sure they don't have to find the same link in rats. And it's not just once but time after time after time. It's the same with those mice over there." Dick pointed to two mice that had their heads placed inside a glass container, and into this container smoke was being pumped. "They're being forced to inhale smoke from cancer sticks."

"Cancer sticks?" enquired Alice.

"Fags," clarified Dick. "Everyone knows these days that they cause cancer."

"So, they are trying to prove that cigarettes are *still* bad for people?" – Alice offered for affirmation.

"No! There, they are trying to prove cigarettes aren't bad for people. You see, that experiment is being backed by a tobacco company, and they are desperate to disprove the link between cigarettes and cancer."

Alice noticed a rat with a tube implanted into his head. "What are they doing to him?" she asked.

"He's undergoing cocaine experiments," replied Dick. "I'm not sure why. Perhaps it's something to do with addiction, or the effects it has on the need for food. Who knows. Your guess is as good as mine. One thing you can be sure about, is that it is needless and cruel. But some bright spark of a student is gonna earn a few brownie points for it. Take that mouse over there for example; every time he takes a drink from that water spout he gets an electric shock. So in the end, he stops drinking."

"But he'll die if he stops drinking," Alice said.

"That's most probably the idea behind it – to find out which is stronger: the basic need for food or the basic function of avoiding pain."

"I hope you don't mind," began Alice tentatively, "but what is being done to you?"

"I'm on a full cholesterol diet," replied Dick.

"Why are they doing that to you?" asked Alice.

"They're trying to induce heart disease," explained Dick.

"You seem quite well," Alice surmised.

"Yeah, I don't feel too bad, actually," said Dick, musingly. "I should also be grateful that they're using this method and not an alternative."

"Why? What other methods are there?" asked Alice.

"Well, can you believe this? They actually clip some of the arteries round the heart, so reducing the blood flow, and therefore meaning to duplicate the problem of furred up arteries. It's crazy."

Alice heard a commotion coming from the other side of the room. "What's happening there?" she asked, but as soon as Alice looked she could see for herself. In a box was a ferret, and the people standing by it had just thrown in a mouse. The ferret immediately attacked it, and in a matter of seconds had killed it.

The people removed the dead mouse, and in its place they threw in a rat. The ferret went straight for the rat. The rat tried to run away – it obviously didn't want to fight – but, as they were in a box with high sides, there was no escape. They fought; both plunging their shape teeth into one-another.

"Ferrets being ferrets," began Bill, "I'd say that it's execution time for that rat."

"Bill!" exclaimed Alice.

"I'll let you know now," said Bill, "it's more than you can afford."

"You're so insensitive!" said Alice.

"I've never been one for kid gloves," said Bill.

"What? Mittens?" asked Alice.

"And what's inside them," continued Bill, not hearing her question (as now he spoke more as if to himself than to Alice). "I don't need it, you hear me, I don't need it."

Bill was a strange case, so Alice decided to leave him to his ramblings.

"Why's that man filming it?" asked Alice, turning towards Dick.

"Most probably so he can take it home and impress his friends," he answered.

The people removed the dead rat and then placed a rabbit in the box with the ferret. The rabbit kept jumping up every time the ferret went for him. The ferret lunged straight for the rabbit's eye and bit in deep. There was a high squealing noise. The rabbit started to kick, spin round, and jump – all in an attempt to shake off the ferret. But the ferret was adamant and wouldn't release its grip. Finally, the rabbit gave in and stopped his struggle. He lay there, motionless, except for an occasional body-twitch. The ferret still held its jaws tight.

"Wow! his teeth have gone right through its skull," said one of the men.

Eventually, the ferret let go. The rabbit was still alive, and every now and then the sides of its body gently rose: finding enough strength and will to inhale another draught of air, holding it, then letting it escape – not knowing if it could be reclaimed again. The rabbit was still fighting – fighting against that slow coming but inevitable fate.

"You should be ashamed of yourself," Bill told Alice.

"But it's not me that's doing all this," pleaded Alice, as she started to cry.

"It's okay," said Dick reassuringly, "we understand really. You're only human." He then added, "Would you like a handkerchief?"

"If we could get out of these cages, we would gnaw you down to the bone!" added Bill. He then unsheathed his long sharp teeth. "It's only what you deserve."

Alice knew it to be wrong, but she did so dislike Bill. "If you did get out of your cage," she said to herself, "I'd grab you and kick you straight out of the room."

"I *will* get you," said Bill, who then twitched his nose and laughed.

Then a guinea pig, who had been sitting quietly nearby, spoke: "He doesn't understand."

Alice went over to him, relieved to have an excuse to leave Bill, "What do you mean 'he doesn't understand'?"

"That this is our lot, that this is our station in life," said the Guinea Pig. "This is what we were meant to do. So therefore we should do it without complaint. Look at my kind, they've even called us guinea pigs. They had been using us as guinea pigs for so long that they decided they might as well call us guinea pigs."

"But not all guinea pigs are used in experiments," said Alice. "My best friend Vicky has two guinea pigs as pets, and I'm quite sure she doesn't do experiments on them."

"Well then they're not real guinea pigs and therefore have no rightful claim to the name," said the Guinea Pig indignantly. "But they are animals, and God made all animals for humans to use as they wish. The only reason animals are in the world is for the benefit of humans, now you can't deny that."

Alice had to think about this; she couldn't believe God would have done that; she couldn't believe God would see the things she had seen as acceptable. But if God didn't agree with it, way on earth didn't he do something about it.

Just at that moment Bill broke into song:

"The animals went in two by two,
 Hoorah, hoorah,
 The animals went in two by two,

Hoorah, hoorah,
But Noah and his wife over slept,
So under the waves they were swept,
And that was God's plan
To see the end of Man."

A shiver ran down the length of Alice's back. In the next moment Bill had leapt from the back of his cage...

Bill was quickly scurrying along the landing of Alice's house. He entered her bedroom and jumped onto her lap as she sat at the window day-dreaming. Alice turned to face Bill; upon which cue, he threw himself at her face.

...and hit hard against the front of it.

"Your friend Vicky is even guilty," said the Guinea Pig. This remark aided Alice in thinking of an answer to the Guinea Pig's previous remark about animals being created solely for the use of people.

"But some animals are of no use; some are actually a nuisance – like fleas," said Alice. "When my friend Vicky got fleas, she hated—" it suddenly dawned on Alice that she had promised Vicky she would never tell anyone about her fleas.

"Yeah, a lice *is* a pain," heckled Bill, as he scratched in the direction of Alice. But she paid no attention to his remark.

"If humans *wanted* to use fleas I'm sure they could find a use," said the Guinea Pig, before turning away from Alice and hence indicating his wish to say or hear no more on the subject.

Alice thought it very uncivil of the Guinea Pig to shun her like that, so said aloud (but as if speaking herself), "What a silly thing to say, that God created animals just for people's benefit."

Then a tiny mouse, from inside a lower cage, said, "God might not have done such a thing, but humans have certainly done it for themselves."

"What do you mean?" enquired Alice.

"Well, what am I?" the Mouse asked.

"A mouse of course," answered Alice.

"Wrong; I'm an oncomouse, patent number 4736866," was the Mouse's (or should I say Oncomouse's) curious reply. "God didn't create us oncomice, humans did; they genetically created us, and they only did that so we would be of some service to them. You see, all oncomice develop cancer within ninety days of birth and then not long after that we die. We are just a tool that is manufactured to fit the requirements. It's a very lucrative business this patenting of new animals. Just imagine coming up with a new animal that all vivisectors want but no-one else can manufacture due to the copyright. The mouse on my left is a hairless-mouse. He was invented so people can test hair restorers. And the mouse on my other side is a wool-mouse. The scientists hope to use the idea behind him to increase wool production."

Unknown to Alice, Bill, in his cage just above her head, had managed to turn himself round and was putting his tail out between the bars. "Such a nice little *human* child," he said, emphasising the word human and timing it so that it coincided with his tail brushing against Alice's face.

The Oncomouse and the Guinea Pig both began to laugh. Alice rose to her feet. And, while trying her utmost not to show the distaste she assuredly felt, said, "I think I should be going now."

"That's right! Turn your back on us!" cried Bill. "I said you didn't care."

"I am sorry for what is happening here," said Alice,

"but it was only yesterday that I knew nothing about any of this. I'm not sure why I'm here, but I think it's to find out as much as I can about you all. And as I have no idea when I'm to be returned home, I think I should keep going. I'm sorry but I don't know what else to do."

Alice, feeling as guilty as Bill thought her to be, moved hurriedly towards the yellow door.

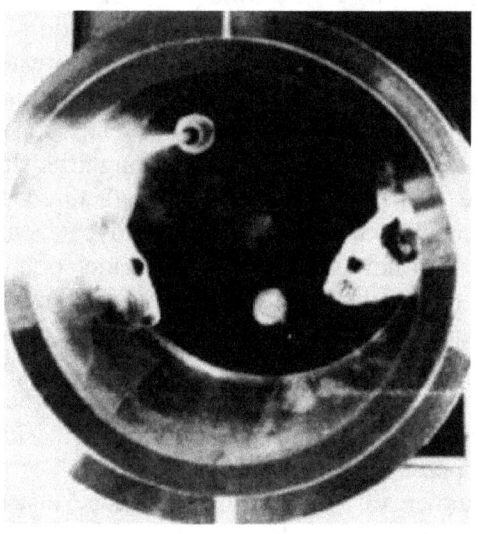

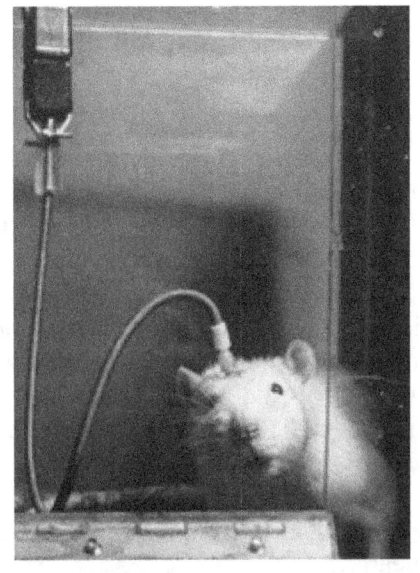

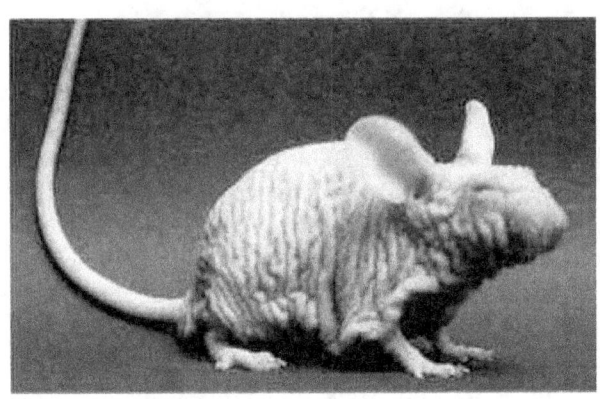

CHAPTER 7

ADVICE FROM A DODO

Alice felt quite relieved when she didn't find herself in a new room but in the doorway again. Though, this time the doorway was different compared with the last time. Here, she could see beyond the doorway and into a long corridor. Along both sides of the corridor were red, yellow, and blue doors; and at the far end was a ladder. Alice noticed that the ladder went up through the ceiling, and as soon as she had seen this she started running towards it. Alice thought the ladder must be a way out.

But even though she was running, the ladder seemed to get no nearer.

"This corridor must be longer than I at first imagined," thought Alice. She continued running, but it soon became quite obvious to her that she was making no headway towards the ladder. Alice became nervous and started running faster, but still she got no nearer. She increased her speed until she was running flat out; but, alas, the ladder remained at exactly the same distance away. She finally gave up and slumped to the floor.

Alice had been lying there for about a minute when she heard someone whistling. On looking up, she saw that it was a Dodo skipping down the ladder and carrying a walking stick under his wing. Even though this was an amazing thing to see, Alice was more surprised at seeing how happy he was. The Dodo didn't seem to have a care in the world.

"Hello there my friend," said the Dodo, when he

caught sight of Alice.

"Hello Sir," returned Alice, just managing to find enough breath to speak.

"And what brings you here?" the Dodo asked.

"I don't exac—" (she had to breathe in) "—actly know."

"Well, I'm just passing through, on my way home," said the Dodo. "I've just been told I'm to meet someone there that I haven't seen for a long time."

"I wish I could," said Alice.

"Why, what is the problem?" asked the Dodo.

"Well, it's this doorway – or is it a corridor – well anyway, it's a long way and I can't get to the end of it," said Alice.

"The exact term for it is corridorway," informed the Dodo.

"But why can't I get to the other end?" asked Alice. "I've been running but haven't got anywhere."

"Mmm, that is a problem," said the Dodo. "You've been, what is known as, running to stand still. Just be glad you're not in the corridorway which makes you leap a mile in the wrong direction, or the corridorway where it's one step forward and two steps back. All are problematic problems when one is trying to go forward."

Alice felt he wasn't taking her exactly seriously. And her suspicions were confirmed when he started trying to see if he could move forward by skipping once forward then twice backwards.

"Sir," called Alice, for she feared that if she didn't stop him he would disappear back up the ladder, "I was wondering..." (Alice was going to ask him how come he was so happy, but thought better of it.) "I was wondering how you managed to skip down that ladder. It did look difficult and dangerous."

"Yes! A death defying feat!" exclaimed the Dodo

jokingly, while swinging his walking stick above his head. "But no, seriously," he continued, returning to his composed fashion, "I would've understood it, if you'd described it peculiar; but dangerous or difficult – no, it's easy really."

"Is it?" asked Alice.

"Of course – I just use my death defying feet," replied the Dodo.

Alice forced a smile. "Why do you carry a walking stick, but not use it?"

"Because it's a lame stick?" guessed the Dodo. "Or, it only becomes a walking stick when I do use it? I give in. Why?"

"I don't know," Alice had to admit.

She then asked, "Why is this place so confusing? I don't just mean this corridorway, but also the fact that I can't turn round and go back the way I've come, and that even though I enter and leave each room by the same door I always enter a different room."

"Ah, that's because you are in the Caucus Maze, my dear," said the Dodo.

"The Caucus Maze?" enquired Alice.

"Yes, a strange place it is indeed," said the Dodo mysteriously. "It causes people to keep going backwards and forwards, and as soon as you start to run you stop. It's a place where nothing seems the same twice, and where the answers to questions are questions. It's a puzzle of a great magnitude – the deeper you go into it the more puzzling it gets, and the more puzzling it gets the greater is the urge to go in deeper. And, as you know to your own cost, it is full of problematic problems. Nothing can be taken for granted; every turn you make, there will something there to bar your progress; you cannot rely upon anything. The unexpected is all you can expect. It's a place where laws are broken, and codes are ignored – a place without love, rules or an end. And, unlike the conventional maze that lets you in easily enough but makes it hard to escape, the Caucus Maze isn't only hard to get out of, but also, for the majority of people, difficult to get into."

Alice felt quite dizzy after the Dodo's description, but managed to say, "I don't know how *I* got in, but I must be in pretty deep."

"You're not the kind to get in deep," said the Dodo. "You have all the signs. But I sha'n't go into that now. We still have your little problem to solve. Let's see, your legs run but your body wo'n't move forward. Mmm, ca'n't you walk, dear?"

"Of course I can," answered Alice.

"Well, I suggest you walk twice as slow as that," said the Dodo. "In fact, pigeon steps would be perfect. Then I'm sure you wo'n't have any further problems."

"Sir, why do you speak in that way?" Alice ventured to ask.

"Ca'n't help it," answered the Dodo, "but I'm managing better than I normally do."

The Dodo then started looking at Alice quite intently.

"Anything wrong, Sir?" she enquired.

"What's..." the Dodo hesitated, "what's your name, my dear?"

"Alice," she replied.

"What?!" screeched the Dodo.

"Alice," she repeated.

"What are you doing here?" the Dodo screeched again.

"Finding out—" but Alice was interrupted before she could get any further.

"Oh no! It mus'n't be so. Go back. You must go back!"

"I told you, I tried that before, but I wasn't able to," said Alice. "Anyway, I've come so far already."

"Believe me, you haven't seen a fraction of it!" cried

the Dodo.

"But shouldn't I at least see what I can?" remonstrated Alice.

"No – no, this is wrong," said the Dodo, despondently.

"But only a small wrong, surely," said Alice.

"Oh, I know," said the Dodo, quite dejected. "But it does upset me." He then looked upwards. "This is more than just a gambit – it's a sacrifice!"

"Please don't be sad," implored Alice. "You were so happy before you met me. I always seem to say the wrong things to everyone."

"Oh, I can be just as melancholy as all the others here," said the Dodo, "when I'm in my normal place."

"This isn't your normal place?" Alice asked.

"No, and what a mercy that is. But I've still got my own good reasons to be sad," said the Dodo. "Has anyone recited a poem to you yet?"

"Well, not exactly a poem, Bill the Rat did sing a short song," said Alice. "I didn't like it though."

"Then I think a poem is long over due. Do you want to hear a poem?" the Dodo asked.

"Okay," replied Alice.

A whole minute passed before the Dodo said:

"FINISHED."

"That was a very good poem," said Alice, trying to be polite.

"I haven't started yet, that was just the title," said the Dodo, with a smile. He then proceeded with his poem:

"'Twas finished, time for sticking hour,
   As wether and wedder had the weight,
   The middlings caused the scour,
   And the smothers escaped.

Beware the Jabknacker, my son,
The jaws bite hard, the hands reach far,
You, the next Dodo bird, don't shun,
The power of the harbourer.

For many years we roamed our land,
Where fear was unknown to us,
But all was soon to change,
Exsanguination with a cut.

As stumpy legged, flightless birds,
No tricks, or queues were needed,
Our beating hearts turned slowly blue,
With every flame they extinguished."

"Well, what did you think of it?" asked the Dodo, once he was finished.

"I don't mean to be rude," began Alice, "but I'm not too sure what it meant. Though it did appear to be of something quite unpleasant."

"That's perfectly all right my dear," said the Dodo, "as I can only take the responsibility for the rhyming."

"Oh the rhyming was nice," said Alice.

"Yes, I'm afraid the reasoning leaves a lot to be desired," said the Dodo. "Anyway, I'll be on my way now. And don't forget: pigeon steps."

The Dodo turned and continued along the corridorway (but not skipping this time, Alice noticed).

CHAPTER 8

CAT AND MUSTARD

*(The second and third rooms in this chapter
contain the actual dialogue used by the
vivisectors while filming their own activities.)*

So Alice began pigeon stepping along the corridorway, and indeed it did work. She was slowly but surely making her way towards the ladder.

Alice had got about half way when she heard a lot of banging and crashing. It was coming from behind a yellow door. The noise made Alice wary, so instead of going straight in she opened the door slightly and peeped in. Almost immediately, an old man dressed in a white coat rushed to the door, and prevented Alice from seeing inside.

"No admittance! No admittance!" the Old Man cried.

"Why not?" asked Alice.

"Because I said so," the Old Man replied.

"I'm not a four-year-old, and I don't think answers like that are answers at all," said Alice, in her most grown up manner (which mainly consisted of holding her left hand in her right hand and placing them firmly on her stomach while keeping her elbows in close to her body).

"If you're not four you can't be much older than five," said the Old Man, "and that makes no odds to me."

"I'm much older than five," said Alice, not wanting to give her actual age away.

"I can guess your idea of much," said the Old Man;

"you most probably think a day is a long time."

Alice had to admit to herself that the day had seemed to have lasted for a long time; but then also, she felt a lot older than she had yesterday. "Actually, I'm nearly fourteen-and-a-half," said Alice, almost as if she really believed it to be true.

"So you're not just ugly enough," remarked the Old Man.

"Ugly enough for what?" enquired Alice.

"To sweep my chimney," the Old Man replied. "But, like I said before, I don't need my chimney swept."

"But I don't want to sweep your chimney," said Alice.

"Oh, I see," said the Old Man. "Well, here's ten new pence; now, be off with you. But don't think the world owes you a living, my girl. And money doesn't grow on trees either, no matter what you might think."

"I don't want money," said Alice; "I came here because I heard banging coming from in there, and I just wanted to see what was happening."

"That banging isn't coming from here; it's coming from the next room," said the Old Man.

"What are they doing?" asked Alice.

"*I* don't know; it's got nothing to do with me," replied the Old Man; "just as what I'm doing here hasn't got anything to with them or you. We are very private people."

Just then Alice heard another bang come from inside the room. "Can I just pass through your room, so I can go into the next room where the noises are coming from?" asked Alice. "I must know what they're up to."

The Old Man gave Alice a confused look, then said, "You dullard, those noises came from the room you're already in."

"No they definitely came from—" Alice began, but then realised what was happening.

"Look little girl," the Old Man said condescendingly, "I'm a very busy person with important work to be done. I don't know why I'm even standing here wasting my time talking to you; you've disturbed me enough already and to be honest child, I just don't want the likes of you in here. And that's final."

"How do you know what I'm like?" said Alice, stalling for time, and so enabling her to look over the Old Man's shoulder and into the room.

"I know many things," replied the Old Man; "I'm not stupid you know. I wouldn't be doing this job if I was."

While Alice had been looking over the Old Man's shoulder she had noticed a framed certificate on the wall. It had written on it 'The Wellcome Gold Medal'.

"Excuse me Sir," said Alice, pointing to the award, "but what is that?"

"Ah! that," said the Old Man, suddenly filled with pride, "that's my..." (he paused for effect) "Wellcome—" but before he could finish his sentence Alice had thanked him for his kind offer and walked in straight past him.

The Old Man looked annoyed.

"Sorry Sir, but you did ask me in, didn't you?" Alice said very innocently. "I am *truly* interested in the great work you are doing here."

"Are you really?" he asked.

"Oh yes, Sir," grovelled Alice some more, and feeling proud of her clever deception.

"Well, you can stay if you just sit over there and remain quiet," said the Old Man. "Because children should be seen and not heard – even if they are nearly fourteen-and-a-half."

Alice didn't like this, but nevertheless agreed with him, then went and sat down. She also didn't like the way he seemed to be taking the mickey out of her 'nearly fourteen-and-a-half'. But why had she said fourteen-and-a-half in the first place. Because even though she wasn't sure how old she really was, she was clearly not fourteen-and-a-half.

"I think first," said the Old Man, breaking her chain of thought, "I should introduce myself: I am Ratty."

"That's a strange name," remarked Alice.

"Oh, it's not my real name," Ratty began explaining, "it's a nickname. It's a reference to my hair." He scuffed up his indeed scraggy hair. "But I don't care; at least I look the part. Also, I believe it has a different meaning in some faraway part of the world. By the way, are you an orphan?"

"No, why?" said Alice.

"Oh no reason, just thought you might be," replied Ratty. "Right then, so what were we doing?"

"We weren't doing anything."

"Weren't we, how boring."

"*We* weren't, but you were."

"Was I?" Ratty was silent while he thought to himself. "Oh yes, that's right, somebody was spying on me from the door."

"That was me," said Alice.

"It was?"

"Yes, but you invited me in."

"I did?"

"Yes, to show me what you were doing in here."

"That's right, what I was doing in here." Ratty pondered for a couple of seconds.

"Yeah," he said, then went over to his bench, still not sure what he was supposed to be doing. He looked at his assistant who held out a cat for him to take. A light seemed to come on inside Ratty's head, and he took the cat, quite eagerly.

Ratty gave the cat an injection to make it go to sleep. Alice noticed how much his hand shook while he did this. It wasn't because he was nervous, but because he was old. On looking up at his face, Alice realised he wasn't just old but extremely old.

"How old are you?" asked Alice.

"Older than my teeth, whippersnapper," replied Ratty.

"Well, so am I, dinosaur," said Alice.

Ratty returned his attention to the cat on his bench. He shaved the top of its head, sliced open the skin with a knife, and then, using a hand drill, started to bore a hole straight into the cat's skull.

Alice felt as if she was going to be sick, but remained seated.

Once the drilling was completed, Ratty got a tube and pushed it into the cat's brain. "I'll have to put this one to one-side until it wakes up," he said, turning to Alice. "I have one here that's now awake which I prepared earlier." He gave Alice a wry smile, as he believed he had said something she would appreciate.

Alice, who didn't acknowledge his remark, asked, "How many of these experiments have you done?"

"Oh, too many to give you a definite number," Ratty replied. "Let's just say I've been doing these experiments for about thirty years."

"You must have learnt a lot in that time," said Alice

"Oh yes, but you can never stop learning," said Ratty. "You see, my experiments are about putting different substances into cats' brains and studying the effects. So you see, the amount of different substances you can try is limitless. Today the substance I am using is – er – mustard."

Ratty then (using the cat he had prepared earlier which was by now fully conscious) injected mustard down the tube and into the cat's brain. He placed the cat inside a metal cage and got ready to observe the effects and write them down.

After about a minute, parts of the cat started

shivering, which soon spread throughout its whole body. After a while the shivering turned to a vigorous shaking. The cat started to miaow, normally at first, then as the cat miaowed more and more the length of the miaow became unnaturally long. Then the cat started growling and yelping. It began to pant, dribble, and twitch its ears. The hairs all over its body stood up on end. The cat retched and then suddenly started leaping up and down and getting very excited. Then, as suddenly as it had begun, the cat calmed down. This was soon followed by it being sick, and wetting and messing itself. The cat charged blindly ahead and hit against the side of the cage. It then leapt up and clung to the roof of the cage and started biting at the wire meshing.

Alice couldn't watch any more and ran out of the room.

She didn't find herself back in the corridorway but in another room that had more people dressed in white coats. None of them had seen her enter the room, so Alice decided to hide in a corner and watch what they were doing.

It then dawned on Alice that she was now in the room where all the banging and crashing must have been coming from. "There doesn't seem to have been any trouble here," thought Alice to herself, as she looked around the room. There didn't seem to be anything broken or even out of place.

Alice noticed that one man was holding a video camera and filming the others about the room. All their attentions were focused on the table in the centre, upon which, seemed to be a monkey lying down. Alice couldn't be sure it was a monkey because its head was inside something that looked like a helmet. Its arms, legs, and body were all strapped down.

The people stepped back from the table. The monkey wriggled about in his restraints trying to free himself, but, as Alice could see, he had little chance.

Suddenly, there was a loud bang! – Some large metal object had smashed with a huge force into the monkey's head. Alice felt her body leap into the air. But the monkey's body could only shudder within the confines of the straps, as the tremor passed through his fragile bones like a shock wave.

The monkey now lay still, after the initial jolt. Alice remained in her corner dumbstruck. She wanted to leave, but was too frightened to even move a finger in case she was seen.

A man went over to the monkey. He lifted up one of the monkey's arms and started waving it to the camera.

"That's him waving," said the Cameraman. "As you can see the monkey is awake, moving all extremities." At which, the man with the monkey disdainfully lifted and let drop the animal's arms and legs. "That's his trainer," continued the Cameraman, "who taught him to do all these tricks." The other man began laughing at the Cameraman's comment.

"Cheer leading over in the corner..." started the Cameraman, as he began swinging the camera across the room.

On hearing this, Alice's heart missed a beat. "They know I'm here," thought Alice to herself, as she waited for the camera to fall upon her. But to Alice's surprise, it didn't, it stopped at a different corner of the room.

"...we have B10," continued the Cameraman. "B10 wishes his counterpart well. As you can see, B10 is alive."

Alice looked at this dark corner of the room; and B10, as they called him, was another monkey. He was seated in a baby's high-chair, and was placed so he could watch all the proceedings. He was slumped to one side – obviously weak and dejected from what had already been carried out on him. He looked up as all the attention of the room was placed upon him, but that was all he could manage.

The Cameraman then said, "B10 is watching, and hoping for a good result."

The people set up the apparatus again and repeated the head smashing experiment on the monkey strapped to the table. After the monkey had received this second blow to the head the people started to remove his restraints. The helmet had been hit with such a force that it had become stuck to the monkey's head and the people couldn't pull it off. So they started hitting it with a hammer trying to dislodge it. The helmet still proved reluctant so they put a wedge in-between the helmet and the monkey's head and started hitting this with the hammer. In doing this they managed to take off part of the monkey's ear. When the monkey's head did finally become free the Cameraman said, "It's a boy!"

A woman made the monkey sit up so the Cameraman could film him. The monkey was unable to support himself, so the woman stood there and held him, which she did at arm's length. The monkey was slumped forward; his arms were loose by his sides; his head hung down on his chest. Suddenly, his body gave a jolt and his arm shot outward: perhaps it was the monkey's nerves still screaming.

The Cameraman then said disparagingly to the monkey, "Look at the camera, here kitty kitty, say cheese."

The monkey slowly leant back and looked up at the woman. She hesitantly returned his look and said, "Yeah, I *know*," and then gave an insecure laugh. The monkey couldn't hold his head up for long and had to return it to the support of his chest.

"I hope the anti-vivisection people don't get a hold of

this film," was the Cameraman's next remark.

Once again the monkey's body jolted and his arm shot out: perhaps it was those two explosions still resonating inside the monkey's head.

The Cameraman, speaking as if for the monkey, then said, "Let me out, don't look." He knew exactly how degrading the scene within his viewfinder was.

The monkey slowly raised his head again to look behind at the woman holding him up.

"Oh, not again, turn around," the woman said, as she looked down at him. But the monkey held his position longer this time. He kept his eyes on her. His eyes on her eyes. Looking, perhaps, for something that wasn't there.

The Cameraman, once again adding a voice to the monkey's silent plea, said, "You're gonna rescue me from this, aren't you? aren't you? You're gonna rescue me from this." All the Cameraman really achieved (from his efforts to be the joker) was to show how he fully understood the atrocity he and his colleagues were committing – how he believed it possible for the monkey to be thinking those things – how he could see it in the monkey's expression. He also showed his callousness.

Alice, still in her corner, was shaking all over. She started crawling towards the door, trying to avoid being noticed, but someone saw her and shouted. Alice quickly rose to her feet and ran for the door. The others also started shouting and ordering her back, but Alice was already gone.

Oh, another room, and more people standing round a table, and yet another animal on top of it.

Alice was still shaking. She just wanted to lie down and cry her heart out.

"You're gonna rescue me from this, aren't you? aren't you? You're gonna rescue me from this." She could still hear those words inside her head.

Alice looked up and saw that the animal on the table was a dog lying on its back. She instinctively imagined it to be Mary lying there. Perhaps one reason for her doing this was the familiarity of such a position – the surrendering of the dog's self either to a stronger force or to be petted. And the vulnerability of the position is so obvious as well, with the belly and neck completely exposed, the lack of mobility, the eyes hidden, and the awkward legs sticking aimlessly into the air.

Out of the people standing around the table one seemed to be the instructor. And this instructor was about to give a demonstration to some students.

The Instructor began speaking: "You see he's still anaesthetised, but he's a little bit light. This is a new idea we've come up with – the needle all strapped." The Instructor showed the students a needle that remained injected, with the aid of strapping, into a vein in the dog's leg. He pressed the catheter. "Just give him another FCC."

"We put this around the ankle," said the Instructor, as he wrapped cord round the dog's back legs. He then started to bend the different joints of the dog's leg. "Is that the ankle? I don't know. No, that's the ankle. Where *is* the ankle on a dog?" The students laughed at his remark and one of them said something that Alice couldn't hear. "Don't you tell me; you don't even know if it's a male or a female!" the Instructor said in answer.

He then tied the dog's two back legs to the two bottom corners of the table, and its two front legs were tied down along the sides of its body.

"See how that sticks him up, that makes a very solid chest to work on," said the Instructor.

Just then the dog gave a short whine, but no-one said

anything. The dog then gave another short whine, and this time it was accompanied with head movements. It happened repeatedly, and couldn't be ignored.

The Instructor placed his hands on the dog's chest, and said, "That's hiccups, mostly." He then discreetly injected more anaesthetic.

"Right," began the Instructor, "what I'm gonna do now is a tracheotomy. I'll cut into the dog's neck and insert a tube. All right, you just pick it up," (he pinched a bit of skin from the dog's neck), "and give it a little nip, like so; place the scissors under the skin and push, okay and cut. See very little bleeding, very little."

There was now a cut about three inches long. The Instructor then put inside the wound an instrument (which was, two prongs that opened and shut like scissors). He opened out these prongs so that the flesh inside the wound opened up. He repeated this again so to make the wound deeper. He then placed two of his fingers into the hole and pulled more flesh apart.

The dog started to whine as the Instructor continued to pull apart the flesh until it was the same width as the original incision he had made in the skin. The dog whined again.

"This is reflex," was the Instructor's explanation.

The dog lay there with a gaping hole in his neck, and whined piteously. The whines weren't short whines like before but long – long stretched out whines. They changed tone; they went from a high wispy sound all the way down to a low guttural sound. The whines pleaded; they expressed the pain, the helplessness, the confusion, the resignation, the pain, the pain, the pain.

"That's reflex," the Instructor said again.

"No! He's awake!" screamed Alice. "Oh stop. He can feel it!"

Everyone in the room looked at Alice.

"Please; he's crying," implored Alice.

No-one said anything.
What could she do?
She ran out of the room.

Alice entered the next room at full speed. The room was in darkness, and Alice had reached the middle of the room before she realised she couldn't see where she was going.

Her body was shaking and her legs felt wobbly, so Alice sat on the floor to try to calm herself down. She placed her hands firmly over her eyes. "You're gonna rescue me from this, aren't you? Aren't you? You're gonna rescue me from this." Those words still spun round her head, as real as when she had first heard them. "You're gonna rescue me from this," – she heard them again; they seemed so real.

Suddenly, Alice removed her hands from her eyes. She wasn't sure now if those words *were* in her head, or actually coming from somewhere to the side of her. She looked over to her side and saw a cage. She could hear a soft whining sound, but the darkness hid the cage's occupant.

"Whatever is in there sounds very unhappy," thought Alice to herself. "I bet its story is as horrible as all the rest." Alice sat there quietly as the animal continued its languid whine. Alice put her hands over her ears trying to cut out the sound.

"I don't suppose I would be of any use to it," Alice thought to herself, as she stood up and walked slowly towards the door.

Checking herself on the very edge of the door step, Alice added, "But once I go through the door I won't be able to come back, and then I'll never know if I could've helped it. I'll just go back and talk to it; that can't do any harm."

So Alice walked back a little way into the room. She didn't want to get too close to the cage, as she was afraid of what she might see there.

"Hello," Alice said tentatively.

"Hello," replied the animal from inside the cage.

"I'm afraid I can't see you too well, what sort of animal are you?" asked Alice.

"That's right, you don't see me too well," replied the animal feebly. It had to pause for a few seconds before it could continue. "I'm a dog." It paused again. "What are you yourself?"

"Oh, I'm a kid," Alice replied enthusiastically, feeling that perhaps things weren't going to be as bad as she had first expected them to be. So she ventured further: "Don't you feel well?"

"No, not well at all," answered the dog.

"Have you been experimented on?" asked Alice.

There was a silence, until the dog finally replied, "Yes."

"Oh, I am sorry," said Alice. She then reluctantly added, "What sorts of things have they done to you?"

"I've been radiated," said the dog.

"What's that?" asked Alice.

"I don't know," replied the dog, "but that's what I've heard them call it."

"Have you looked in a mirror to see if you look different?" was all Alice could think of to ask.

"I know what it does to me," the dog began, "it makes me sick a lot, gives me terrible headaches, makes me feel so weak that I can't even stand, and yes I do look different, horribly different. I've got huge lumps all over my body."

Alice wished she hadn't mentioned the mirror.

"But the thing that makes it worse," added the dog, "is that they did it to me while I was pregnant."

"Oh! You're expecting pups?" cried Alice joyfully.

"No, I've already had them," answered the dog.

"Have you really!" Alice said in surprise. "Little puppies are so cute. I wish I could see them." Alice then realised she hadn't heard a single noise from any of them "Why! they are very quiet for puppies. When my Mary was a—"

"That's because they're dead," interrupted the dog, before Alice could say any more.

Alice felt sick and wished she would think before she spoke. But the dog didn't take it badly and just continued:

"You see, because of the radiation I didn't produce any milk. My puppies kept on sucking though, and because of this I became ever so sore, but no matter how much I tried I wasn't able to push them away. But gradually, one by one, they died."

"Didn't anybody come here to feed them?" Alice asked.

"No, I haven't seen anyone for days," replied the dog.

Alice remained silent as she pictured to herself the horrible thing that had happened there. The dog finally broke the silence:

"So what have they done to you?"

"Oh nothing as yet," Alice replied.

"That's good to hear." The dog paused. "Sorry, but what is your name?"

"Alice."

"My name's Pearl."

"Oh, so they give you names down here?" said Alice

"No, down here they just give you a number. Pearl was my name before I came here, when I lived with a human family."

"You mean you were somebody's pet dog before?" said Alice, quite shocked.

"Yes, that's right," Pearl replied.

"Did they send you down here because they didn't want you anymore?" enquired Alice.

"Oh no, they loved me and I loved them." Pearl paused for a moment. "You see, they had gone out for the day, but were unable to take me, so I was left in the back garden. Me, like the fool I am, had to get out. And it was while I was walking the streets that two men grabbed me and shoved me into the back of a van. I then ended up here."

"You were stolen!" said Alice aghast.

"Yes."

"That's terrible!" Alice then remembered about her Aunt whose cat just disappeared one night. They had thought it must have been run over or perhaps gone off chasing another cat and become lost. But now, Alice realised that it could have been stolen and ended up in a place like this.

"I wish I could open that cage and let you out," said Alice, quite upset.

"That's okay, don't worry about me now, just look after yourself," said Pearl as bravely as she could.

"I'm afraid I've been no help to you at all," said Alice. "I can't even give you any water." She then remembered she had an old sweet in her pocket. "I could give you a fruit-polo, if you want. It's a bit fluffy though."

"Not much good to me; I've got no teeth," said Pearl, who then quickly added in her reassuring tone, "but you have helped me immensely. It's been so good to talk to a friend."

By now, Pearl was feeling tired. The exertion of speaking so much had taken it out of her. "Hopefully I'll see you again sometime."

"Yes, I hope so, too," replied Alice.

"Goodbye then," said Pearl.

Alice reluctantly said, "Goodbye." She didn't want to

leave.

"And thank-you," added Pearl.

As Alice moved slowly towards the door, she felt quite pleased with herself for stopping and spending a few minutes with Pearl.

Alice didn't pass straight through the door and into another room – nor did she step back into the corridorway – but found herself, once again, stuck in the normal doorway.

"I think I've thrown away my chance of getting out of here," said Alice to herself. "I'm never going to find that corridorway again."

Realising the significance of being in the doorway, Alice began looking around for the Kitten.

"How's it going?" a familiar voice asked, on cue.

Alice looked up and saw the Kitten slowly appearing before her eyes. "Horribly. I don't like it here at all," she complained. "Everything's so sad. And frightening. When I think of the things now, it's hard to believe they actually happened. There was this cat that had mustard—"

"I know exactly what you've seen," interrupted the Kitten, "but what are your opinions?"

"My opinions?" queried Alice.

"Yes, on the things you've seen," said the Kitten.

"I think they are absolutely terrible," said Alice, "and utterly cruel."

"What about the people?" asked the Kitten.

"They *are* strange," said Alice. "I can't understand why they do these things, but I suppose they must have their reasons."

The Kitten stared at Alice with what seemed a quizzical look, so Alice added an explanation. "These people are doing cruel things, but as they are clever and skilful, they must know what they're doing." Alice pondered for a second. "But then again, no matter what the reasons, it's got to be wrong to do those horrible things to those animals."

"Mmm, I would have to disagree with you about them being clever and skilful people," said the Kitten. "That is perhaps the misconception many others have also made. Take Ratty for instance, he should have retired years ago. Instead he's bumbling along doing worthless work badly. If he was in a proper medical profession he wouldn't be allowed to carry on. He can't even keep his hands still, and his memory is going. And what is the point of those experiments? I've no idea.

"And those people doing head impact experiments on monkeys – I don't think they can be described as clever or skilful; they're just out to enjoy themselves. They are meant to be measuring the effects of an impact to the head. So what do they do? – they get out a hammer and start hitting against the helmet. Now any results they may have obtained are rendered useless.

"Now I don't have to tell you how absurd it was for that instructor to put the dog's whining down to reflex. We both know that the dog was awake and quite aware of what was being done to him. Crying is not a reflex but a conscious expression of pain. There's just no such thing as a whine reflex."

"Er..." Alice began hesitantly, "what did the instructor mean when he said the student didn't know if the dog was a male or a female?"

"Well, he must have asked the students earlier if they knew the sex of the dog, and they couldn't have been able to tell him. But seeing as the instructor himself was referring to the dog as 'him', I think that can mean only one thing."

"What?" asked Alice.

"Well you see, these dog's aren't only used once,

they're normally used all day by different people for different demonstrations. So, if the dog is a male, but now looks like a female, we can make a guess at what's happened."

Alice remained silent.

"These people are just failures that didn't have the brains or the skill to work in a proper medical field," continued the Kitten. "People in the medical profession are there to heal and save lives; only vivisectors set out to cause pain and take lives."

"I know," said Alice; "the things I have seen make me feel sick. I can still see them in my mind. I wish they'd go away." Alice could feel a cry coming on, but managed to suppress it.

"I know it's distressing," said the Kitten, "but vivisection thrives on the public's ignorance. These things have to been seen; just reading or being told by someone is not enough. Even seeing photographs is really only half the picture."

"You seem to know so much," said Alice.

"That's because I've seen the devil," said the Kitten.

Alice didn't understand what he meant by this but didn't like to ask. "When you get older, you're going to be a truly wise old cat."

"No, I'll never become a cat," said the Kitten, quite sadly.

"Why not?" asked Alice.

"Oh – er – why should I become a cat?" began the Kitten, shaking off his melancholy. "I want to be something bigger than a cat. A cat's even smaller than a kitten, so where's the sense in that?"

"Where's the sense indeed," remarked Alice.

"No, I want to become something big," continued the Kitten, "perhaps a cataclysm, or a catalyst – anything, rather than just a cat."

"Oh I see," said Alice. "Would you like to become a

cat's cradle? Now that would be nice."

"Yeah," said the Kitten, with a slight smile.

"No, that's two words," said Alice. "How about cat's-paw?"

"Alice, I think—" began the Kitten, before being interrupted by her.

"I know; it's a hyphenated word. Well, if that's not allowed, how about catfish?"

"No, I think it's time—" the Kitten tried again.

"Caterpillar!" interjected Alice. "That's it, that's the longest yet. You will become as big and wise as a caterpillar."

"Alice!" demanded the Kitten.

"Oh, I don't want to go on," pleaded Alice, "I want to stay here with you. I feel safe with you."

"There's still more for you to find out," said the Kitten. "Like you've still to meet the Tester and the Researcher."

"But why me?" remonstrated Alice.

"'Why me' – 'why me' – 'why me'," the Kitten repeated over and over again, until finally fading out – along with the Kitten himself.

Alice immediately felt lonely, and couldn't stop her eyes brimming with tears. "I wish I could change into something else," thought Alice, trying to console herself. "Perhaps I could change into a bird and fly away, or change into a mouse and scamper out undetected."

After considering this idea for a moment, she soon added, "Oh no, with the things I've seen today, this is the last place to be an animal. No, I think it's safest I remain just as I am."

"Why you?!" screamed the Kitten's voice suddenly into Alice's ear; which was then followed by the Kitten himself, like a visual echo. "Because they'll say: 'she's sacrosanct', 'such things shouldn't happen to her', 'it's a disgrace', 'it shouldn't be allowed'. But you're nothing in comparison. Just one from the millions is of infinitely greater importance than you." With this the Kitten disappeared.

Alice moved forward and left the doorway.

CHAPTER 9

THE MAD DRUG ASSOCIATION

On entering the room, the first thing Alice noticed was the smell of food. It made Alice feel extremely hungry. She then noticed a long bench in the middle of the room. At this bench were two people sitting drinking tea. They were both wearing white coats so Alice approached tentatively. She guessed that they must be the Tester and the Researcher.

"Perhaps they'll ask me to join them for breakfast," thought Alice – but without holding out much hope.

"Please take a seat," said the Tester, turning to Alice. She was so surprised at his hospitality that she just stood there.

"Don't stand!" snapped the Researcher.

Alice looked around for somewhere to sit but couldn't see anywhere. She noticed that at the other end of the bench there appeared to be an armchair that was facing in the other direction.

"It would be rude to sit in the armchair with my back to them," thought Alice, "but if that is the only place to sit then that must be where he meant me to sit. I could turn it round, but I don't think it's right to move other people's furniture about. And anyway, they must have put it like that for a reason."

All Alice's dithering was for no purpose because when she got to the armchair she noticed it was already occupied. In it was a person curled up and fast asleep. As the person wasn't wearing the customary white coat Alice wondered if the Tester and Researcher even knew that he was there.

"Excuse me, but I can't find anywhere to sit," Alice called back to the other two.

"Don't wake him up," whispered the Researcher. "Come over here."

Alice walked over to them and repeated that she couldn't find anywhere to sit.

"That's because there *isn't* anywhere to sit," said the Tester.

"So why did you tell me to take a seat?" asked Alice.

"Because that's what I always say to visitors," said the Tester, "and normally they enter into the spirit of things and take it literally and pick up a stool and walk off with it. That's always good for a laugh; we never tire of that one. If you can't laugh what can you do?"

"That might be why you haven't got any stools left," said Alice, choosing not to answer his question.

"Well then," said the Researcher, "it must be time for us to send out invitation cards for a 'bring-a-stool' party."

"And I bet," said the Tester, beaming, "that one of that crazy bunch would actually bring a sample of his own faeces." At this they both went into hysterics.

Alice thought them an unlikable pair, but knew she would have to put up with them if she wanted to find out more.

"What is it you both do?" she asked.

"I find new drugs," said the Researcher, "new drugs to treat— I mean cure, all the ills of man. There's a pill for every ill."

"And I do tests on those new drugs (and all manner of other substances, I might add) using the LD50 test," said the Tester.

"What is the LD50 test?" asked Alice.

"Oh, very important," said the Tester.

"I didn't mean that," said Alice."

"You should say what you mean and not what you

please," said the Tester.

"I'm sure I do both," said Alice.

"You mean, you mean what you please?" the Tester asked.

Alice thought about this. "No, I don't think I do."

"Why not?" asked the Tester.

Alice found the Tester annoying, but persevered: "LD50 tests, what is it they test for and how do you do them?"

The Tester smiled then said, "They test for a result and I do them well."

Alice could see that he could avoid answering her questions no matter how she worded them. "Why won't you answer my questions?" she asked.

"If they're your questions that means they're not mine, so why should I bother answering them," said the Tester.

"Please yourself," said Alice, seeing how futile the situation was. She then turned to the Researcher. "Do you answer other people's questions?"

"Do I look silly?" he replied.

"So you don't?"

"Did I say that?"

"I think you did."

"But you aren't sure, are you?"

"No," was Alice's only answer. She then asked, "Do you know what LD50 is?"

"Is that a trick question?" replied the Researcher.

"I don't think so."

"But you aren't sure, are you?"

"No," said Alice resignedly.

The Tester then clapped his hands loudly, and said, "Hey, let's play a game of cards."

"I'd rather not, actually," replied Alice, who was feeling quite fed up with the two of them.

"Yes, and whoever loses has to talk about what they

do," said the Researcher.

Alice realised she wouldn't get a better opportunity than this to find out what they did. "Okay," she said, "what shall we play?"

"Can you play Snap?" asked the Researcher.

"Of course," replied Alice, "anyone can play Snap."

"How do you play it then?" asked the Tester.

"Well, each person takes it in turn to lay a card down, and when a card is laid on top of a card of the same value the first person to shout snap wins the pile of cards."

"Okay, let's start then," said the Researcher.

Everything had been going fine with the game until the Researcher shouted snap for a ten-of-hearts being placed on top of a queen-of-hearts.

"That's not snap," remarked Alice.

"Yes it is, they're both hearts," replied the Researcher.

"But it is only snap when they are of the same value – that's the rules," demanded Alice.

"No, they're your rules, not mine," said the Researcher.

"That's cheating," said Alice.

"Cheating is when you break the rules," the Researcher informed Alice, "and I haven't done that. I'm just not following your rules."

"Okay, but from now on we can all say snap for cards of the same suit," said Alice.

"Fine by me," said the Researcher.

The game continued smoothly for a little while, but then the Tester decided he would say snap for a seven-of-clubs and a two-of-spades.

"That's not snap!" shouted Alice.

"Who said?"

"We did."

"Well I've just decided you can say snap for cards of

the same colour," said the Tester.

"You can't just keep changing the rules through the game," said Alice.

"When are you going to understand, that there are no rules," said the Researcher.

"You can't have a game without any rules," said Alice, "that's silly."

"It doesn't seem silly to me," said the Tester.

"But rules are what makes one game different from any other game," explained Alice. "If there are no rules how do you know which game you are playing?"

"Exactly; total freedom," said the Researcher.

So the game continued in this vein, with the pile of cards never building up, because snap was being shouted nearly every go. But Alice stuck at it, and just tried to be the quickest. She so much wanted to beat them both.

"Thirty love!" the Researcher shouted, after he had laid down the ace-of-diamonds.

The Tester and Alice both looked at him for an explanation.

"That's the second ace I've served," explained the Researcher.

The game went on and on, and no-one came even near to winning. Alice was finding it extremely tedious, and it was difficult for her to keep her full attention on the game. The other two were as keen as ever.

The Tester had just laid the king-of-spades, and now it was Alice's turn. She put her card down, and it was the queen-of-diamonds. The Researcher was just about to lay his next card, when Alice shouted:

"Check-mate! It's check-mate! My queen has check-mated your king. I win!"

The Tester and Researcher both looked down at the pile of cards.

"Is she right?" the Tester asked.

"Of course I'm right," said Alice. "And now you can tell me about the LD50 test."

"I was going to tell you anyway," said the Tester. "But I just needed a bit of mental stimulation first." He dropped his cards onto the table. "I hope you've got your clever head on for this. Right, sitting uncomfortably? – then I shall begin." The Tester wriggled in his seat, gave a little cough, and then begun. "LD50s measure the toxicity of drugs or substances that people are likely to come into contact with. They find the amount that would be dangerous. Everything needs testing, and the public rely upon me. I'll explain what I'm doing as I do it, that way I won't have to think twice."

The Tester took a mouse from a cage. "The animals we use are mainly mice, rats, rabbits, birds and fish but we also sometimes use dogs, cats and monkeys.

"To start, fill a syringe with the substance," he said accompanying his actions. "Then you put the nozzle into the mouse's mouth and push it down its throat until it's..." he paused as he twiddled the nozzle about, "until it's... there, inside the animal's stomach, then you just inject the substance straight into the stomach." He placed the mouse back in its cage.

"You would then repeat this same dosage on the rest of the mice in your batch. This first dosage is made purposefully high so insuring it will kill the majority of the mice. A period of fourteen days is allowed to see how many die. If it *is* more than fifty-percent you then have to get a new batch of mice and give them a reduced dosage. Fewer will die this time in the fourteen days, but if once again it is more than fifty-percent you get another batch of mice and decrease the dosage again, and again, and keep on decreasing the dosage until only fifty-percent of a batch die. Then, *voila*, you have the LD50 number."

"The LD50 number?" enquired Alice.

"LD50 stands for Lethal Dose 50%," said the Tester. "Which means, in simple terms, the single dosage that will kill fifty-percent of a population."

"So you keep using new batches of animals until fifty-percent of a batch die, no matter what you're testing?" asked Alice.

"Well yes, if you want to find the number," said the Tester.

"So you could find the LD50 number for – say – water?" asked Alice

"Of course, anything," said the Tester.

"But the dosage would have to be extremely large to kill them," said Alice.

"I suppose it would," replied the Tester.

"But wouldn't it just be the large amount of water that's killing them?" said Alice, confused at the Tester's oversight.

"The LD50 is a toxicity test," said the Tester, equally confused at Alice's inability to grasp such a simple concept.

Alice couldn't tell if he was being serious or just silly like before. "What happens to the survivors of each of the batches?" asked Alice.

"They're terminated," said the Tester, "they are of no further use."

"So a load of animals are killed for just one substance," said Alice.

"Terminated is what we prefer to call it," said the Tester. "But think of what we're finding? See those rats over there; they're being force-fed lipstick. The dosage we're up to is 25grams; that's 25grams of lipstick for every kilogram of body weight."

"But people don't eat lipstick," Alice felt she had to point out.

"They might accidentally," said the Tester. "Do you

take sugar with your tea?" he then asked.

"I do. One please," replied Alice eagerly, because if she wasn't going to eat she could very much do with a drink.

"That's a good thing," said the Tester, "because if you took 52lb. it would kill you."

"That must have taken a long time to find out, *and* a lot of animals," said Alice.

"There is another test you can do, and it's quicker," said the Tester, with renewed enthusiasm, as he took an unused rat from its cage. He then inserted the tube, injected the substance and put the rat down on the bench. The rat first started trembling, then writhed in agony.

"It's obviously a harmful substance!" cried Alice, "can't you give it something to take away the pain?"

The Tester gave Alice a stern look and said, "I test for toxicity, not pain killers; that's the Researcher's job."

"Oh," mumbled Alice.

"Yes," said the Tester. "You see, the Researcher would give the rat something toxic then administer his new antidote. If the rat stops writhing then it's worked, if it doesn't then it's back to the drawing board."

All this time, the rat's writhing had become more vigorous.

"Haven't you seen enough?" enquired Alice. "Why don't you put it out of its misery?"

"Oh, can't do that," said the Tester, "it would invalidate the result."

"Doesn't it upset you to see it in so much pain?" asked Alice.

"Emotions are unscientific," said the Tester clinically.

The rat continued its writhing until finally it died – much to Alice's relief.

"That's called the Writhing Test," said the Tester, proudly. "You give the animal an excessively large dose and measure how much it writhes."

Alice was astounded: "Is that scientific?!"

"Of course," said the Tester, "I'm a scientist, aren't I? I wouldn't be allowed to test drugs if I wasn't."

"But why wasn't that rat sick?" asked Alice. "If I ate something bad I'm sure it would make me sick."

"Oh, rats can't be sick," said the Tester, "nor mice, nor rabbits."

"So why use them, if they can't be sick like a person?" asked Alice.

"Well, they show up many side-effects in drugs," said the Tester, "so of course we're gonna use them. Anyway, you can use dogs when testing for vomiting."

"Don't the dogs bite you when you try and force things down their throats?" asked Alice.

"No doubt some dogs would," began the Tester, "but why do you think we use beagles, huh? Oh, they are such placid, trusting, and loving animals that it doesn't matter what you do to them, they'll never turn on you. They never bite the hand that bleeds them."

"Is it necessary to use animals to test drugs?" asked Alice.

"Sure it's necessary. We can't use people, can we," replied the Tester.

"There must be better ways?" said Alice.

"There's nothing better than what I do," claimed the Tester.

"So when a drug is toxic or shows side-effects in an animal, the same will happen in a person?" enquired Alice.

"Of course," acknowledged the Tester.

"Why 'of course'?" asked Alice.

"Because animals are like us," he replied.

"But if animals are just like us, it can't be right to kill

them," said Alice.

"Oh, of course it is," said the Tester.

"But you couldn't kill people for these tests?" Alice continued.

"No, that's right," he replied.

"So why is it okay to kill animals but not people?" persisted Alice.

"Because animals aren't like people," said the Tester without hesitation.

The Tester then said he had to go and check on some rats whose fourteen days were up. So, while he did this, Alice began looking at the assortment of papers on the table in front of her. There were many. One was headed 'Clioquinol'; it listed all the animals used, along with the different problems some of these animals had encountered from taking the drug.

The Tester then called across the room to Alice. He was holding up five dead rats by their tails. "Do you know what these tell me?"

"No, what?"

"That the LD50 for Isoprenaline is 800mg."

Alice immediately looked back down at the papers spread out in front of her. She started rummaging through them, and soon found the one she was looking for; it was headed 'Isoprenaline' and gave the LD50 number for rats as 50mg.

"This here says it's 50mg," Alice told the Tester. "But your result is 800mg. Why is there such a difference when rats were used both times?"

"Well, they *were* different strains," pondered the Tester, as he began walking back across the room.

"So one rat can give a different result to another rat?" asked Alice.

"Yeah," mumbled the Tester. "Or I suppose it could have been that they were feed different food. Or perhaps different bedding was used."

"Even that can change the results?" said Alice.

"Oh yeah," said the Tester.

"The test can't be much good if so many different things can affect the results," said Alice.

"The test no good!" shouted the Tester. "So – what – you're calling my job pointless? Look kid, I do many tests on all different types of animals, and work it out from there. See these results here for methylfluoracetate," (he gave the longest name he could find), "they give the LD50s for different animals." He tossed Alice a sheet of paper which had the following written upon it:

mouse. 6.7
rat. 3.5
rabbit 4.0
guinea pig . . 0.4
cat. 0.3
dog. 0.15
monkey . . . 11.00

Alice looked at the sheet and thought of all the animals that had died to give those results. She then looked at all the varying numbers.

"See," said the Tester, "I do thorough tests before I think of a result."

"So what is the result," asked Alice.

"Don't know yet," answered the Tester. He then quickly changed the subject: "Want a drink?"

"Yes please," replied Alice, as she was quite dry from all the talking she had been doing. "I don't think I've asked so many questions in all my life," Alice thought to herself, "but it's hardly surprising when everything's so confusing."

The Tester handed Alice a bottle. There was a label on it, and Alice knew she should read it before taking a drink. The label was covered in long words, and Alice had no idea the meaning of any of them. Also, there were many different numbers on the label (so many so, that I believe if Alice could have added them up, I'm sure she would have got an E on her calculator). But Alice could read and understand one part, the part that said 'Contains arsenic'.

"You're trying to poison me!" cried Alice.

"No I'm not," replied the Tester, evidently taken aback by her accusation. "Why do you say such a thing?"

"There's arsenic in my drink!" she shouted.

"Oh, is that all," said the Tester, with a sigh of relief; "no need to worry about that."

"But arsenic's poisonous," said Alice.

"You've been watching too many old murder films," began the Tester. "It's a myth you know. You see, I've given huge quantities of arsenic to sheep, and it's had no adverse effects on them."

"Oh dear," was all Alice could say.

"Yes I know, it's terrible how they try and deceive us," said the Tester. "I think it's a conspiracy, you know. Because, you won't believe this, but I've being doing tests on Penicillin and I tell you..." he looked around making sure there was no-one else listening, "...I tell you, it's fatal for guinea pigs. Yes fatal. And do you remember the big furore about Thalidomide. That drug wasn't to blame; it couldn't have been. All the normal animal tests were done before it was put on the market, and it proved safe. And then afterwards, I tell you, I don't think there was an animal in the world that wasn't tested with it, and still it proved safe – well, all except the New Zealand white rabbit – but anyway, can you see now, how it must've been something else that was to blame. Actually, I've heard from some quarters that iatrogenicity is on the up. I don't exactly know what it is, but I bet it was to blame. Or it could've even been..."

Leaving the Tester muttering to himself, Alice turned away and looked at the Researcher. He was sitting with his feet up on the table and his eyes closed. Alice thought of him actually trying to find drugs for people to take, using animals.

"I suppose you have the same problems?" Alice asked the Researcher.

"No, I don't have any problems," he replied, without opening his eyes, "I'm able to release papers all the time."

"What do you mean?" asked Alice.

"Well, if you want to get on in this job," began the Researcher, now opening his eyes, "you have to keep releasing papers as regular as clockwork, showing the new things you've discovered. And I tell you, doing it this way works a treat."

"Does it?" enquired Alice.

"Of course it does," said the Researcher. "How many different animals do you think there are in the world?"

"Quite a lot," replied Alice, not wishing to play guessing games.

"More than that," said the Researcher. "So just think of the situation: I want to find out if such and such a drug does such and such a thing; all I have to do is persevere until I find the animal that gives me the result I want. It's just perfect."

Alice was shocked.

"But it's not just new drugs I have to come up with," continued the Researcher, "I also have to create the situation where I can start testing out new drugs – like, say, making an animal arthritic. And just look at cancer and heart disease – animals don't suffer from any human cancers, and heart disease just doesn't exist in the animal world. So, before I can even start trying drugs I have to imitate these conditions in the animals."

"Like clipping veins around the heart?" said Alice.

"Yes, that's right, ingenious isn't it," said the Researcher.

Alice didn't answer in agreement, but instead said, "I've just thought of something that dogs don't suffer from like people."

"Oh yes, what's that?" asked the Researcher.

"Colds," replied Alice. "I've always wondered why whenever I've had a cold, Mary, my dog, has never caught it. Even when it's been a really bad cold and all my family has caught it, still Mary hasn't caught it. So it must be that she *can't* catch our colds."

"Yeah," said the Researcher. "Anyway, as I was saying, you have to imitate the problems. With cancer you've got various options. You can treat the animals own type of cancer. This can be done by waiting for the cancer to form naturally, but this is impractical as it takes too long and there isn't any certainty that the animal will get cancer. So what you do is you give the animal cancer producing drugs, then you start trying to combat the cancer with drugs. Another way is to actually graft tumours onto the animal. Or now, you can give them human cancer genes."

"How many do you give them?" enquired Alice.

"How ever many it takes," said the Researcher. He then smiled as he added, "But not so many that you have to get signed consent forms from them before you can carry out any further work."

He then picked up a mouse from a tray and laid it in the palm of his hand. "Just think, this little blighter could hold the key to breast cancer; you never know, you know. One day we will find a cure for cancers."

How have you given her breast cancer?" asked Alice.

"It's not a her it's a he," replied the Researcher. "You see, the drug I'm using to induce the cancer has no affect on female mice but it does on the males." He then replaced the mouse in the tray.

"To simulate arthritis, I inject air into their joints."
He showed Alice some other mice in a box; they had
massive lumps over their bodies.

"Is that like arthritis?" Alice asked.

"It might be," he replied.

"Is it right to cause them pain when you're unsure?"
she asked.

"Ah, but how do we know they feel pain like we
do?" Here the Researcher picked up a rat and dipped its
tail into his hot cup of tea. The rat fought to free itself.

"See, it felt nothing," said the Researcher. "But I
think it would've preferred coffee though."

"I hate seeing animals being hurt," said Alice.

"Oh, you'll grow out of that soon enough," said the
Researcher.

"I think we should give her some Crestfallen," the
Tester butted in.

"Me too," agreed the Researcher.

"Crestfallen, what's that?" enquired Alice.

"Well, it knocks you for six and makes you feel
really low, so then when you finish the course and stop
taking it you feel ten feet tall," explained the
Researcher.

"No, I'd rather not, thank-you," said Alice, "but I
wouldn't mind a cup of tea."

"Oh, you won't want this, it's camomile," said the
Tester.

"Why is a raven like a writing-desk?" the Researcher
then asked.

Alice shook her head; she had heard too many riddles
already.

"I know! I know!" cried the Tester excitedly. "Can I
answer it if she doesn't know?"

"Okay," said the Researcher.

"Because there's a B in both," was the Tester's
answer.

"No, wrong," said the Researcher; "it's that they both produce papers."

"I think they both should be made to shut up," Alice remarked.

"No, doesn't mean that at all," said the Researcher, who then took out his watch. "My, is that the time; I think it's time for you to leave."

"Why, what is the time?" requested Alice.

"Late!" snapped the Researcher.

"Yes, and my watch says it's ten past late," added the Tester.

Alice spun round on her heels, and made for the door. "I hope I never have to see those two again."

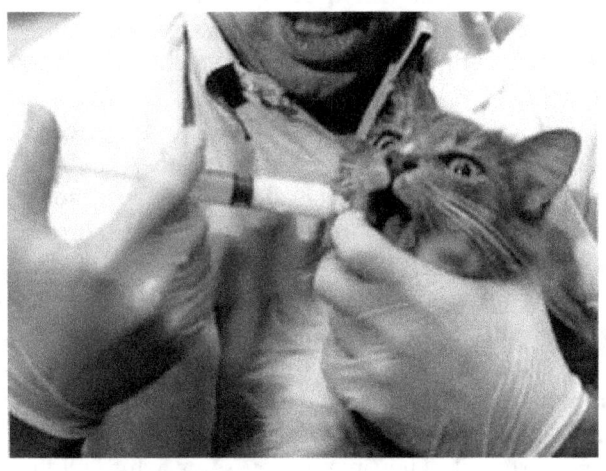

CHAPTER 10

A REUNION

When Alice reached the yellow door she paused before going through. "I don't seem to be getting anywhere, and I'm definitely no nearer home. I just seem to be going in and out of this yellow door. Perhaps it would've been better if my name was Dorothy instead of Alice."

She went over to the red door, wondering if it might now be unlocked. She tried to open it, but, alas, it was locked.

"Why is this door always locked?" Alice said to herself.

She walked across to the blue door and tried to open that one. It swung open easily, and to Alice's surprise she was looking straight at herself. Just across the threshold of the door, looking just as surprised as herself, *was* herself. The room, this other Alice was standing in, was exactly the same. There were the same white walls; the same table; the same apparatuses; the same two stools; same chair; same cages, with the same animals in them; same pieces of paper on the table; same headings on those papers... But the two people in there were different. They wore they same white clothes and did they same things, but they weren't the Tester and Researcher she had just met in her room. Alice looked back up at her other-self, who did the same. Even though it was definitely herself, the other Alice's face seemed somehow wonky, like her face did in photographs. Both the Alices simultaneously raised their hands to the door and slammed it shut.

Alice stepped sideways to the yellow door, and proceeded to open it and walk in. She was horrified at what she saw. On the floor was a pig, and the man standing next to it was blowtorching it all along one side. The pig squealed as the roaring flame ran up and down its body. The pig's skin turned brown and then started blistering. The blue flame of the blowtorch looked cold but the white sparks within it – the ignitions of the flesh – told a different story. The skin started blackening, then cracked apart. The skin hardened and came away from the body, so that when the pig moved it looked like an armadillo.

The man turned off and put down the blowtorch. He then picked at the hard blackened skin – exposing the flame spared pinkness underneath. He looked at Alice and said, "What's up, don't you like streaky bacon?"

Alice turned round and ran out of the door. She found herself in another corridorway. But instead of a ladder, this corridorway had a flight of stairs at its farther end.

"Oh thank God!" cried Alice, who was quite shaken by what she had just witnessed. She started running towards the stairs.

"No, no. Pigeon steps," said the Dodo, who had, seemingly, sprung from nowhere.

"Oh, hello again," said Alice. "I thought you were going home."

"A slight misunderstanding," said the Dodo. "All to do with the word reunion."

"Was it?" remarked Alice.

"Yes, but it wo'n't do it again," replied the Dodo. "Once a word has been found out, there's no hiding place for it."

"No," said Alice, out of politeness.

"So what about you and vivisection?" asked the Dodo.

"Oh, you wouldn't believe what I've seen..." And here Alice gave an account of all the things she had seen.

When Alice had finished, they both remained quiet for a few moments, until the Dodo sighed and said:

"I know. It's silly, terrible, laughable, tragic, and plain deception. If vivisection were stopped tomorrow it would never be introduced again because no-one would ever be able to find an argument supporting its introduction."

"That's very well put," said Alice.

"I can only take the credit for the plagiarising," said the Dodo. "Anyway, I suppose I shouldn't detain you any longer."

"Yes, I had better be getting on," agreed Alice, still eager to get up the flight of stairs.

"Mmm, getting on indeed," said the Dodo reflectively. "As a matter of interest – how old are you these days?"

"It's strange," replied Alice, "but I'm not sure. Earlier, I thought I was fourteen-and-a-half, but I know I can't be that now."

"You could be," said the Dodo, "it all depends on the decided approach to solving the problem. But no, let's see: 73 divided by 98 equals 0.745. So that's 74.5%, and 74.5% of an hour is 44.7 minutes, and 70% of a minute is 42 seconds. So you are 7 years, 364 days, 23 hours, 44 minutes, and 42 seconds. Easy!"

The Dodo then glanced at his workings out again. "No, that's not right, that's assuming—"

"Shouldn't the seconds have gone up?" interrupted Alice, as she didn't want him to start more calculations.

"Sorry? What was that?" asked the Dodo.

"The seconds, they would have gone up in the time it took you to work out and say how old I was."

"Not the way I worked it out, they wouldn't," said

the Dodo. "Anyway, do you know at what o'clock you were born?"

"I think it was three o'clock in the morning."

"Exactly three o'clock?"

"I don't know," replied Alice.

"Okay, never mind," said the Dodo. "Right, so we had 75.2% of—"

"Dodo?" interrupted Alice

"Yes?"

"Can we do this another time?"

"Don't you like number crunching?" asked the Dodo.

"I do, but I'd just like to do it some other time?"

"Well, it ca'n't really; but I understand what you mean. I was getting carried away, sorry."

The Dodo looked at the flight of stairs. "If you see Professor Egghead, give him a narrow berth." He turned away from the stairs and continued along the corridorway. "Bye then, my dear."

"Goodbye," said Alice.

"And don't forget all that you learnt in those lessons I gave you," the Dodo shouted back, as he disappeared from sight.

"What lessons?" thought Alice to herself, "I don't remember any lessons. But if he did give me lessons, I'm afraid he must be a poor teacher because I can't remember a single thing." Alice pigeon stepped towards the flight of stairs. "And who's Professor Egghead?"

CHAPTER 11

PROFESSOR EGGHEAD

Alice looked up the dark stairway and could see a light at the top. Hesitantly, Alice ascended the stairs. When she reached the top, she cautiously poked her head out of a little hole; whereupon, she found herself out in the open-air. She sniffed in its freshness, and then climbed out of the hole. She looked up into the sky; it was clear blue, with just a few small fluffy clouds spotted about. The sun was up high and shinning down on her. It felt so warm and comforting that it made Alice shiver slightly as she felt the coldness leave her body.

The hole, Alice had just emerged from, was on top of a hill, and even though it was only a small hill Alice felt she was looking upon the whole world. She indeed had a good view of the wonderful landscape laid out before her. There were isolated trees and bushes scattered about; there were beds filled with bright flowers of all the colours you could imagine; there was a fountain with cool shimmery water; and in-between all these things, was lush green grass. But the things Alice admired the most were the beautiful red roses that seemed to be everywhere. Alice had always thought them such noble flowers.

In the distance there were fields: each a different shade of green or yellow. The fields were made square by the partitioning thick hedgerow.

Now looking beyond the fields, Alice took in the ocean; before finally resting her eyes on the horizon.

With her eyes still fixed on the horizon, Alice said dreamily, "This is strange; I wonder where I am now?"

She then began twiddling her toes in the soft grass.

Alice came out of her reverie when a slight movement caught her eye. On looking, Alice saw what she thought looked like a person sitting on top of the farthest hedgerow. With a clear lack of alternatives, Alice decided she would walk in that direction to see who it was.

What a pleasant journey it was, with the sun, the flowers, the quietness, the freedom. Alice even began singing to herself; she actually felt happy.

Alice had got about half way along her journey when she heard a small cry of: "Ouch!" She looked around but couldn't see anyone, so resumed walking.

"It's bad enough you treading on me, but not even apologising!" said the small voice again.

Alice looked down to where the voice seemed to have come from, and saw two small frogs.

"Oh, I am sorry; I didn't mean to," said Alice.

"Perhaps you should watch where you're going in future," said the Frog.

"I will do, for sure," said Alice. She had turned ready to carry on with her walk when the Frog spoke again:

"You stepped on him as well, you know." He pointed to his companion. "Aren't you going to apologise to him?"

"I didn't know I had," said Alice; "he didn't say anything."

"That's because he hasn't got a tongue," said the Frog. "We're completely identical apart from that. Everything exactly the same. We're one of a kind and two of a pair. Except he hasn't got a tongue, so that's why he didn't say anything."

"And you make up for it," thought Alice, before she said, "Why hasn't he got a tongue?"

"We're as alike as two fleas on a dog," continued the Frog. "Eh, what did you say?"

"Why hasn't he got a tongue?"

"Catching flies, you know," the Frog said.

"No I don't," replied Alice.

"He was a tadpole," was the Frog's next remark.

"Well I know that," said Alice.

"I only kiss princesses, you know," the Frog informed Alice.

"I'm not a princess," she replied.

"You said that a bit too fast, for my liking," complained the Frog.

"I – am – not – a – prin – cess," said Alice, slowly.

"Very quick!" remarked the Frog.

"I'mnotaprincess," Alice spurted out.

"I think we should be off now; I hear a storm brewing in the distance." And with this, both frogs hopped away.

Alice continued on her way, and eventually made it to the hedge (which she now realised wasn't a hedge at all, but a wall covered in ivy). She was now able to see who was sitting on top of it: he was an old man in a cloth cap, he had white hair showing, and the glasses he had on made his eyes small. He also wore a burgundy cardigan, and even had a pair of matching burgundy slippers on. With all these things, plus the fact that he had such a genial face, Alice came to the conclusion that he must be friendly.

Also on the wall was a raven. Alice thought it strange that the bird stayed there while a person sat so close.

"Hello little girl," the old man said, "and what brings you out here?"

"I'm looking for Prof. Egghead," said Alice. She had no idea why she had said this; she knew the Dodo had mentioned a Prof. Egghead; but why should she be looking for him?

"I'm pleased to tell you," began the old man, "you are speaking to him: I'm Prof. Egghead. But please, call me Frankly."

"Sorry?" said Alice, not sure she had caught his name correctly.

"Not sorry," replied Prof. Egghead, "Franky."

"Oh," mumbled Alice.

"And whom have I the pleasure to be talking to?" asked Prof. Egghead.

"My name's Alice."

"Ah yes, a sweet name for such a sweet girl."

Alice was surprised by Prof. Egghead's manner: it wasn't what she had come to expect: he was friendly. And he wore normal clothes: not white overalls like all the others. Alice even thought he looked a bit like her grandad. Also, he grinned so very wide. But yes, that was it – if there was any *one* thing wrong with him – it was that he seemed to smile too wide. So wide, that Alice thought the ends of his mouth might meet behind. "And then," began Alice thinking aloud, "I don't know what would happen to his head. Perhaps it would fall off."

With this, Prof. Egghead leapt to his feet and started to talk very excitedly:

"What did you say? Someone's head has come off? Where? Give it to me. Yes! Give it to me!" His face turned red; he started jumping up and down; and then he roared:

"Off with their heads! Off with their heads!"

The raven remained on the wall throughout the whole of Prof. Egghead's violent display.

Prof. Egghead finally calmed down, and sat back down on the wall. Alice was a little taken aback by this outburst, and also surprised that the raven hadn't flown away.

"That raven isn't scared very easily," remarked Alice.

"Oh him, no," said Prof. Egghead, quite back to his

old self. "He's unflappable."

"Why was you shouting 'off with their heads'?" Alice ventured to asked.

"I wasn't," said Prof. Egghead, "I was saying 'off with their bodies.'"

"No you weren't," insisted Alice, "I heard you say heads."

"Bodies."

"Heads."

"Bodies."

Alice decided to give up the dispute over whether it was heads or bodies. "Sometimes he's just like a wild animal," she thought to herself, "and other times he acts like a child. I wonder what he'll be next?" Then, speaking to Prof. Egghead again, she said:

"Anyway, what's the difference between 'off with their heads' and 'off with their bodies'? They both result in them same thing."

"There's a lot of difference," replied Prof. Egghead, "and that is why I am always careful of what I say. And that is why I said, most assuredly, 'off with their bodies'."

"I can't see there's any difference, either way you end up with two separate halves."

"Yes, but what you take from what and what you leave remaining are very important," said Prof. Egghead, who was now getting fairly agitated.

"Are you sure you mean important?" asked Alice.

"Of course I'm sure I mean important," replied Prof. Egghead.

"Are you sure you're sure?" goaded Alice.

"Yes!" Prof. Egghead said in a raised voice.

"If you are, you are; if you are not, you are not," said Alice.

"Not what?" he asked.

"Important," said Alice.

"Be quiet, you're starting to drive me up the wall," said Prof. Egghead, quite annoyed.

"You were already up there when I came here," demanded Alice. "But I do think you should come down and stand in front of it, as my neck is quite aching from continually looking up at you."

"I've earned the right to sit up on this wall from all the work I've done," said Prof. Egghead. "It's a position of prestige, of privilege." He looked about his surroundings. "I am king of all I survey." He then reeled in his gaze and looked at Alice. "So I don't come down for a little girl like you!"

Alice realised that she would have to be careful, otherwise he wouldn't tell her the sorts of things he did.

"Sir?" began Alice politely, attempting to mollify the situation.

"What?" he replied.

"I just wondered, what the work is, you exactly do, Sir?" She was trying her hardest to be polite, but she couldn't by any means bring herself to call him Franky as he had asked her to.

"Why do you want to know?" answered Prof. Egghead, as a small smile returned.

"Well, I've heard a lot about you," said Alice, crossing her fingers behind her back.

"Like what?" His grin moved to one-side. But it soon disappeared as he started shouting:

"I saw the ivy grow! It's out of control! Cut it back!"

Immediately, a man holding shears appeared. From where? – Alice hadn't noticed. But it wasn't until he had cut the ivy back an inch or so that Prof. Egghead resumed speaking again:

"So what is it you've heard about me?"

"Well, that you do experiments on animals," – was Alice's stab in the dark.

"You've been opening doors, finding trees in forests,

and saying there must be a fire at the bottom of a smoking chimney," Prof. Egghead said, now once again grinning too wide. But Alice was quite careful not to mention the fact.

She also thought he was being silly just to obstruct her. But then, suddenly, he sat up straight, his smile subsided and he said:

"I will tell you what I do; I don't mind telling you. I do many things but the thing I am known for, and for which I think is the reason you are here, is body transplantation. I sever the heads off monkeys and connect them to the bodies of other monkeys. I have won awards for my work: some of the highest accolades."

Here, he paused in his speech, leant forward and offered Alice his hand. "You may shake my hand if you want."

Alice didn't, but thought it best to. While they were shaking hands, Alice could feel how unsteady he was. "It would only take a slight tug and he'd fall, I'm sure of it," thought Alice.

"So you see," continued Prof. Egghead, as soon as they had released hands, "my work might sound horrible but it is for an overall good, and people recognise that fact. Admittedly, I haven't perfected it yet, and most probably never will, but I'm covering important ground for people in the future, who will also work in this field of research.

"It's true, the monkeys don't live very long, and that while they do live, are paralysed from the neck down. But I don't care about that. The only reason they are paralysed is because I haven't worked out a way to rejoin the nerves of the spinal cord. But that's boring. It's much better to go ahead (pun most definitely intended) and stitch heads on bodies. I'm not concerned in the least that they are paralysed, or if their heads swell up, or that they feel pain, or whether they're the slightest bit distressed. I'm doing important work here for mankind. I work for God. Someday people will thank me."

While he said all this, so calmly, so righteously, Alice noticed that he was gradually becoming less and less human.

"Say a genius has a cancer ridden body," Prof. Egghead continued, "and he hasn't got long to live – what a waste of a great brain. But if we could transplant a healthy body to his brain then that genius could go on living. Who knows how long the life span of a brain is; perhaps great brains could be given many bodies and live for hundreds of years. Maybe that will happen to me; perhaps my brain is destined to live for many years continuing its great work. But before I can reach such a pinnacle, I've got to step up my experiments to the next stage: testing body transplantations using humans."

Prof. Egghead looked down at Alice, and said, "I could start work on you if I wanted to; I can do anything. What I say goes. I snap my fingers and you must jump." He turned red, jumped up and started roaring:

"Off with her head! Off with her head!"

Alice stepped back, quite afraid, but restrained herself from running away immediately, so she could say, "I..." She faltered and had to swallow. "I hate you! You're evil!"

Alice turned round and started running back along the way she had come. Prof. Egghead began roaring 'Off with her head' again. While Alice was running she noticed that the red roses were dripping – that the red colour was dripping away from their petals. And underneath, Alice could see, the petals were actually white.

The cries of 'Off with her head' were gradually

becoming more and more distant, so Alice ventured to stop and turn round. She could see Prof. Egghead jumping up and down, and flapping his arms about; but she now noticed two men in white coats running towards her. They were gaining fast.

Alice started running again, but it was quite obvious they would catch her before she reached the hole on the hill. Alice darted round the corner of a hedge, and ran along it, making sure all the time to keep her head down. On finding a gap in the hedge, she crawled in, and concealed herself by pulling some leaves in front of her. Alice peeped out and watched the two men run past. She waited until she thought it safe, then crawled back out into the open. To Alice's dismay, the hill with the hole was still two fields away.

"I don't think it would be safe to go across the open fields the way I came," thought Alice wisely; "I think I'll keep close to the hedges. It might take longer but I can always quickly hide if those two men appear again."

So Alice started following the hedge, and it took her quite out of her way. It wasn't long before she didn't recognise where she was. And walking a bit farther, she came upon a large building.

"Silence in court! Silence in court!" Alice heard coming from inside the building. Alice approached cautiously, and stood outside the door.

"Silence in court! Silence in court!" the person from inside shouted again.

"If he stopped shouting 'silence in court' there would be silence," thought Alice.

Entering the building, Alice found that it was indeed a court of law; and, just at that moment, a lady was getting into the witness stand.

"What have you to say concerning the drug Oxyquinol?" asked the Judge.

The lady shifted her position nervously, then

proceeded to speak: "Oxyquinol. Ban it. It should be outlawed. Nobody, not even my nurse, can understand how much I've suffered these last three years during which my body has been racked by pain. I am aware of becoming weaker day by day. I have pain in my back, my chest, my shoulders, my head, my eyes, my nose, my teeth, my ears. I cannot describe the pain I suffer, and only those who have been afflicted by SMON can know what the pains are like." The lady began to cry, then had to be helped down from the stand.

"A shocking case," said the Judge. "Mrs. Victim wants compensation, so we have to find out who is responsible. Next I call her doctor to the stand."

As the doctor stepped up into the box Alice noticed that he had a big question-mark on his shirt. "I wonder what the question-mark means?" she thought. "He doesn't look like Doctor Who, or even a Witch Doctor." She puzzled over it for a bit. "Why, I don't I think it's possible to guess who he is; he has less clues than when Dad and I played Cluedo, and he made Mr. Black die from natural causes."

"So what was wrong with Mrs. Victim when she first came to you?" asked the Judge.

"Diarrhoea," said the ?Doctor.

"Just diarrhoea," said the Judge; "nothing else?"

"That is correct," said the ?Doctor.

"So by trying to treat her diarrhoea you caused SMON?" said the Judge.

"That is correct," said the ?Doctor.

"Could you describe to the court what SMON is," said the Judge.

"Well, it stands for: Subacute Myelo-optic Newopathy," began the ?Doctor. "It is the poisoning of the spinal cord and the optic nerves; it leads to paralysis of the lower limbs and serious disturbances of vision, even blindness. It can be fatal."

"So you caused all that," said the Judge, "when you gave Mrs. Victim Oxyquinol to treat her diarrhoea."

"That is correct," said the ?Doctor.

"Wasn't it known to cause SMON?" asked the Judge.

"No, it's fairly new on the market," answered the ?Doctor. "And SMON didn't exist before this drug came out."

"So what you're saying," began the Judge, "is that this new drug introduced a totally new disease?"

"That is correct," said the ?Doctor.

"Couldn't you have used an established drug," said the Judge, "that you perhaps knew wouldn't cause such devastating side-effects?"

"I had no reason to suspect it of being unsafe," replied the ?Doctor.

"So why did you choose that drug in particular?" asked the Judge.

The ?Doctor had to think for a minute – obviously mulling things over in his head. "It was written on the side of my pen," he finally said.

"You prescribed something, that you didn't know whether was safe or not, because it was written on the side of your pen?" said the Judge astounded.

"I was told it was safe," said the ?Doctor; "the drug company had sent me a lot of literature about it; it really did seem good. They also sent me a pen with the name on it. So you see, when I was considering what drug to give Mrs. Victim for her diarrhoea, I happened to glance at my pen and that reminded me how much the drug company had recommended Oxyquinol for just such a case."

"You may step down now," said the Judge. "I next call the Drug Company Representative." A confident looking man entered the box. "So it was your company that made the drug," continued the Judge. "Does your company see itself as responsible?"

"Definitely not," the Drug Company Rep. said. "It had been thoroughly tested on animals. Every precaution was undertaken before we let it out on the market. Our results from the animal experiments didn't indicate that there would be any problems with the drug. In that area we cannot be faulted; we tested on a wide range of species, as we always do I might add. No; we are not, in any way, responsible; we did all the right things. It's sad," he said, turning towards Mrs. Victim, "but the unexpected will always happen . . . unexpectedly."

"Very well," said the Judge, "it does seem you did everything in your power to make sure everything was covered. You may step down. I next call the drug tester."

Alice was shocked when she recognised the drug tester as the Tester himself.

"So you were the one who carried out the tests for this drug," said the Judge.

"I did indeed," said the Tester, "and I would like to say, categorically, that I didn't find anything wrong with Clioquinol —I mean Oxyquinol," he added quickly. "It's the same thing, just another name for it," he then explained.

"Clioquinol," repeated Alice to herself, as the name triggered some recollection. "I remember, yes, there was a paper in the Tester's lab with that name at the top of it." Alice then shouted out: "It did cause problems in the animals! I saw his papers. It did cause problems!"

At this point the court erupted into a confusion of noise; everyone seemed to be shouting at once:

"I don't know her!" – "See! See! It was proven to be no good!" – "Preposterous! Absolutely preposterous!" – "But I saw the pictures of all the healthy animals!" – "Corruption!" – "I don't know her! I've never seen her before in my life!" – "They ignored their own results!" – "Deception! Plain deception!" – "It was in all the bumf they sent me!" – "I want an adjournment!" – "How could they go against the facts! How could they expose me to so much torture!" – "Money!" – "They're used to it!" – "I demand an adjournment! I demand an adjournment, now!"

In addition to all this commotion, the Judge was continually shouting: "Silence in court! Silence in court!"

After about five minutes, things started to calm down – that is, all bar the Judge, who thought it was his duty to carry on shouting at the top of his voice. He was even going strong when everybody else had ceased making the slightest sound, long ago.

He did stop, as soon as he realised that once again he was the only one making all the noise.

"Right," croaked the Judge, "as we have had some unexpected evidence, I think this court should adjourn for a period of ten minutes."

After the allotted time, the court sat again to resume the case.

"Obviously the girl has something to say," said the Judge, hoarsely, "and I believe she should be given the opportunity to address it to the court. Also, it has been suggested to me that this court should follow the Shut Your Mouth Rules from this point on."

"What rules are they?" asked Alice.

The Judge looked at Alice sternly, then whispered, "It means no-one must talk. Well, no-one apart from me, but I'll try to talk as little as possible."

"Why aren't I allowed to speak?" asked Alice.

"I have to be fair to both sides," said the Judge, "so if I allow you to talk, it follows that I should also allow the other side to prevent you from talking."

"But how am I going to tell you what I have to say if I can't speak?" asked Alice, despondently.

"Haven't you heard of mime, child?" said the Judge,

in a raised tone. "Now, no more talking, or I will have you removed from this court."

"How daft," Alice thought, "having to mime when I've got so much to say. Like – how stupid the Tester is, how his results for Clioquinol *had* shown problems, how his results are never the same twice, how he doesn't know what his results mean, how crude the LD50 and writhing tests are, how he thinks arsenic isn't poisonous. And the Researcher, who finds what he wants to find, and ignores what he doesn't want to find." Alice let slip an audible sigh. "Not even Lionel Blair could mime all that."

Alice began her arduous task by pointing at the Tester.

"The Tester," said the Judge.

Alice shook her head. She pointed to the Tester again, but this time she also screwed her index finger into the side of her head.

"The *Mad* Tester?" suggested the Judge.

Alice gave a nod. She then started rummaging around inside her pockets, and when she produced her tissues she made her face show delight.

"The Mad Tester sneezed?" guessed the Judge.

Alice shook her head, then wiggled her ear with her hand as she produced a pound coin from her pocket to show him.

"Sounds like coin?" asked the Judge.

Alice shook her head.

"Sounds like pound?" was the Judge's second attempt.

Alice nodded, then placed the coin in the left corner of the shelf in front of her. She put her hand above her eyes, in a seeking gesture, then looked to the right, then straight ahead, then over her shoulder, until she finally looked in the direction of the coin – whereupon, she raised her hands in exclamation. She picked up the coin and tossed it into the air.

"The Mad Tester found," said the Judge.

Alice nodded. She then made out she was holding a small bottle and undoing its lid. Between her thumb and finger she pulled out a small something and placed this something on her tongue. She then drank from an imaginary glass of water.

"The Mad Tester found Oxyquinol," said the Judge.

Alice gave a relieved nod. She continued with the mime by touching her ear again, then placing imaginary things in her arms, until she was holding a great many imaginary things.

"Sounds like armful," said the Judge, who immediately added, "harmful."

Alice gave her rudimentary nod before starting on the next word, which consisted of imitating a mouse, then a dog, and finally a monkey.

"The Mad Tester found that Oxyquinol was harmful to animals," said the Judge.

Alice gave a big nod.

"It's a disgrace!" shouted Mrs. Victim. "An absolute disgrace!"

"Shut your mouth!" bellowed the Judge, who then added a moment later the word 'rules'. "I recall the Drug Company Representative to the box."

The Drug Company Rep. entered the box, oozing confidence.

"So what have you to say to this charge that has been put against you?" asked the Judge.

"Before I answer that," began the Drug Company Rep. "which I will, I'd just like to point out that the girl was totally in the wrong for such an outburst. The law doesn't allow the releasing of any information about a drug company and its products without the company's prior consent. No-one here has any right to know how our drugs are produced, tested, or what results we obtain. Anyway, as I said before, I will answer the charge put against us; we have nothing to fear. She's claiming it was found that the drug was harmful to animals. Well she's right, absolutely, one hundred percent, right. But what does that prove? Everyone knows that different substances affect different animals in different ways. And as humans are animals we also react in our own individual way. Therefore whatever is found out using animals can in no way be equated with what might happen in the case of people. The results from animal experimentation cannot be extrapolated to humans."

Suddenly, someone started laughing. Alice looked around and found it to be the Researcher.

"You may step down," said the Judge.

Alice was dumbfounded. But then something dawned on her. "He spoke! He didn't mime!" she shouted. "What about the Shut Your Mouth Rules!"

"Ah, yes," began the Judge, "er, can't be helped now. But I would like to remind everyone here about another clause to the Shut Your Mouth Rules – the one that states that no-one can repeat any of the proceedings that have occurred here today to anyone outside this courtroom. You may all leave the court."

Alice remained and watched them all leaving. She noticed Mrs. Victim go up to the ?Doctor and say to him, "Doctor, I feel suicidal."

"Take these," said the ?Doctor, as he gave her a bottle of pills; "they should do the trick."

Alice was the last one to leave the court, and because her mind was on other things she didn't notice the two men in white coats approaching her. And before she knew what was happening they had grabbed her, and were dragging her back to Prof. Egghead.

In the clutches of these two men, Alice was despairing at the thought of what awaited her; but then she happened to notice a faint moon low in the sky. Seeing the moon come out before the sun had gone down, cheered Alice up a bit. She always liked looking at the moon, and because it had made such an obvious effort to come up while the sun was still blazing it seemed all the more special. She lifted her head high. For some reason her morale had been bolstered by that thin slice of moon.

Alice was brought before Prof. Egghead, who was looking at his watch. He looked up at Alice: "Did you find my thimble?"

"I didn't know you had lost one," Alice replied.

"You dull child! Of course I haven't lost it!" snapped Prof. Egghead. "I've never had it; but it's out there somewhere, and it belongs to me."

Alice poked her tongue out at Prof. Egghead. He glared at her. Then, extending out his arm to show Alice his watch, he asked, "What is the time?"

Alice looked, and saw it to be a plastic watch for young children.

"I could have a gold one if I wanted to," said Prof. Egghead, sensing Alice's opinion of it; "I *could* afford it."

"What's the point if you can't tell the time?" asked Alice.

"I can; I just want you to realise what the time is," Prof. Egghead replied.

"Well, it's ten-to-two," said Alice.

"Oh no, that's wrong," said Prof. Egghead, who then turned his wrist slightly, causing the hands of the watch to flick from ten-to-two to twenty-past-eight. "What time is it now?"

"What a stupid watch," thought Alice, "no-one would buy it like that." She then told Prof. Egghead the time.

"Good, just as I thought," said Prof. Egghead. "So,

who's been a naughty girl then?" he asked Alice, as he produced a white coat and proceeded to put it on. He then plucked a feather out of the raven and inserted it into the band around his cap. Alice now noticed that there were many other black feathers already there. "—You have," Prof. Egghead finally answered for himself.

"You may shake my hand if you want," said Alice.

"*Your* hand. Ha! she offers me her hand. A grubby little paw. You need to be taught a lesson, my girl. Bow your head."

Alice didn't say anything; she just straightened her back and held her head up. She felt a good couple of inches taller. She could feel her heart beating. She looked skywards.

Prof. Egghead – a rotund, hunched over, old man – felt his bones creak as he looked downwards.

He then noticed Alice's shadow grow and move across the ground. Suddenly, it went dark, and Prof. Egghead looked sideways to see if the raven had finally taken flight.

But, as Alice could see, it wasn't the raven that had caused the darkness, but the fact that the sun had gone down. And now it seemed, Alice thought, that the crescent moon glowed proudly.

The wind started blowing, and Alice could hear the ocean waves sloshing behind the wall. In next to no time, the sea was crashing hard against the wall.

Prof. Egghead started panicking, and was running along his wall. The two assistants were very concerned for Prof. Egghead, and kept telling him to be careful and asking him what they should do.

When first one wave and then another came cascading over the wall, it became apparent that the ocean's intention was to flood the whole area. Even though Alice was nervous she couldn't stop herself from giggling with excitement.

When the two assistants decided to run for their own safety, Alice shouted, "Scramble!" and then, with a spring in her step, trotted all the way back to the hole on top of the hill.

Before going back down the hole, Alice turned round so she was facing in the direction of Prof. Egghead, and, at the top of her voice, started singing:

"Humpty Dumpty sat on a wall,
Humpty Dumpty had a great fall,
All the King's horses and all the King's men,
Couldn't put Humpty together again."

CHAPTER 12

ESCAPE

Alice climbed down into the hole. And to her surprise, she wasn't in a new room but back again at the top of the stairs in the corridorway.

"Does this mean I've finally finished my journey?" she asked herself. "And could it really mean that I'm going home now?" She was truly overjoyed by the idea. So much so, that she straddled the banisters and slid down to the bottom.

Alice began walking along the corridorway. A little way ahead she saw a Coke machine.

"Oh good!" exclaimed Alice. "I'm gasping for a drink." But as she approached the drinks machine, she heard barking coming from behind one of the doors nearby. On opening this door, Alice saw cages full of beagles.

"If I don't take them with me, the people down here are sure to kill them," Alice said to herself. "Wouldn't it be murder to leave them behind?"

To Alice's astonishment, the first cage door she tried – opened. She picked up a beagle and gently held it in her arms. It had been given something and was very woozy. The beagle managed to open one of its eyes to see Alice's soft smile. Alice then realised that she would not be able to carry any more.

"I'm sorry, but I can't carry more than one," she said, as she opened the rest of the cages. "Please try and follow me; I believe I'm getting out of here." Upon which, Alice added to herself, "Even though I'm not sure how I'm going to do it, at the moment."

The dogs followed Alice out of the room and into the corridorway. They walked the length of it right up to the door at the end. On passing through the doorway and entering the room, Alice found herself back in the room where she had seen the pig. This was just as she had hoped, because it proved she was really retracing her steps.

Once all the beagles were in the room, Alice got them to leave by the same door. Some of the dogs needed coaxing as they were afraid of returning to what they had just so recently left behind. Their fears were soon dispelled, once they saw for themselves that it was indeed a different room. They were in the room of the Mad Tester and Researcher. Once again, Alice got them all to turn around and leave by the same door.

Now they were in the dark room where Alice had spoken to Pearl. She went over and entered the cage (as now, no cage door barred her entry). Pearl was lying perfectly still and Alice thought her to be asleep. Alice saw small dark bundles of fur around the motionless dog, and realised that they were her dead puppies.

"Pearl," Alice gently called, but the dog didn't move. Alice bent down and stroked her back; it was indeed riddled with large lumps, but the thing Alice noticed most was that the dog was cold. Alice knew then that Pearl was dead. She placed her head on top of Pearl's head and started to cry.

How long Alice would have remained like that we will never know, because after she had been lying there for a few minutes she heard a voice calling her.

Alice looked up; and for the first time, since returning to the labs, realised that there was no ceiling above her; for now she could see all the stars of the night sky. The voice continued, but from where, Alice could not determine:

"Alice, God cares for the dead, you must care for the living."

Alice knew this to be true so slowly stood up and went through the door accompanied by all the animals.

Now standing beside the bench where the surgical demonstration had taken place, Alice looked at all her dogs and realised just how lucky they had been. They all walked out.

The room where she had seen the monkey having his head smashed in was now deserted. All that was left were the instruments – the tools of the trade. They gave a chilliness to the room. Alice recollected that it was the same feeling she had felt when she had gone to The London Dungeons and seen all the devices used for torturing people in the past.

They turned around and entered the next room.

Once again, there were no people or animals there. Alice stood still, thinking about all that she had seen there, and wondered where they had gone.

The dog that she was holding started whimpering and getting restless.

"He must be coming round," thought Alice, "and I suppose what was done to him is starting to hurt." She looked down at the dog in her arms and noticed that something about him had changed, something in his appearance.

Just then Alice's feet felt wet. On looking down at them, she noticed a shallow pool all over the floor.

"It's coming through the door!" exclaimed Alice, in alarm. "Oh no! it must be the ocean that came over Prof. Egghead's wall. It must have risen so high out there that it has reached the top of the hill, and is now pouring down the hole. It won't take long for it to fill this place!" Alice looked around at the animals. "We'll have to run, we haven't long!"

They all rushed out and found themselves in the first corridorway. Being confronted by so many doors, Alice panicked and became confused; she didn't know which one to take. And there was also the ladder – should she take the ladder? No. But that was it: the ladder had been at the far end, so her door must be the one at the opposite end, and not one of the doors along the sides.

They splashed along the corridorway heading for the chosen yellow door.

On the other side, they were in the room with the rodents.

"Oh dear!" cried Alice, "there are so many cages to be opened, and the water is rising so quickly." As indeed it was, for the water was already up to Alice's ankles.

"Those of you who can swim, please do so; it's not much further," pleaded Alice, as she quickly opened the cages; "and those that can't, will have to get onto the backs of the dogs. Please, hurry!"

Alice was tearing about everywhere trying to assist in the animals' escape. The dog she held let out a piteous whine from the pain he was feeling. Alice glanced down at him and saw now that his eyes were open. She thought his eyes weren't like dog's eyes. She knew it a strange thing to think but was sure of the fact. Also, his whole appearance looked less dog-like than it had the last time she had looked at him. Alice had to put this curious idea to one side for the moment, while she continued aiding the rodents in their escape.

Finally, they were all ready to leave, so waded through the water towards the door.

They passed through the Snakes and Ladders room.

In the next room, as Alice had most dearly hoped for, was her bed.

"Quick, get on the bed," Alice told the animals; "we will be safe from the water there."

The dog's whine, that had by now become continuous, had adopted a strange tone; but Alice, in her pursuit to get all the animals safely on her bed, hadn't had time to even look down. But once they and herself were all safe on the bed, she ventured a look to see what was wrong. To her total astonishment she didn't see so much a dog there but more a sort of baby. A human baby!

"This is indeed strange," said Alice, "but I haven't got time to worry about that now – I've got more important things to worry about. I haven't only got animals to look after, but now also a baby!"

Alice and the animals remained on the bed as the water rose. Very soon the bed was afloat.

"I think we will still have to go back the way I came if we want to escape," said Alice to the animals. She looked at the door they had to leave by. "Though, it is going to be difficult!" said Alice, showing concern. Difficult indeed it would be, because the water was entering and leaving by the same door, causing a whirlpool.

It then hit Alice what the next room was. (It was the room where, last time, she had become transfixed at the sights it had contained; the room she had described as hell.) Alice didn't want to go in there again, but knew she must. She had an idea: she would close her eyes as soon as she entered. She understood that these things had to be seen but she had seen enough, she knew vivisection was wrong, she didn't have to see any more, she knew how bad it was.

So Alice and the animals (that is, the ones who were able to) began paddling. It was hard work, but inch by inch they got closer to the door, until: whoosh! they were shot forward into the next room.

Alice, to her word, immediately shut her eyes. But in her mind she saw dirty, shabbily dressed, thin children in cages. On the outside were people dressed in white coats; and to these people, the children were handing over things – they were giving them their kidneys! – their hearts!

Alice shook her head vigorously. She now saw women handing over dolls to the people in white coats. No, they're not dolls, they're moving, they're alive. They are very tiny babies. The white coated people took the babies from the women; they cut off their heads; they connected the heads to artificial hearts and lungs, keeping the decapitated heads alive. Other babies were cut into pieces, mashed up, spun in a spin-dryer, and pressed to extract the liquid from them.

Alice opened her eyes to dispel the images. The first thing her eyes fell upon was a human leg floating on the water.

Alice wanted to get out of the room as soon as possible. She quickly manoeuvred the bed round so they could continue their journey. She then looked down at the dog-baby she held within her arms, as his crying was still constant. And now, she noticed, there wasn't a hint of dog left; it had completely changed its appearance and was definitely a baby.

Now in the room with the depressed Baby Monkey, Alice immediately pulled him from the ever deepening water onto the safety of the bed. Before saying a word, she put her arm around him and held him close to her. Silent moments passed before she spoke to the Baby Monkey:

"I've just thought of the answer."

"I didn't ask you anything," said the Baby Monkey.

"Do you remember when I met you before," began Alice, "and you said that death was your only answer for getting out?"

"Yes," replied the Baby Monkey.

"Well it's not," she said. "Love is the answer."

Leaving that room, they entered the one with the infected monkeys. Alice opened up the containers and cages that imprisoned the monkeys that were free from infection, but the others she knew she couldn't free.

"I can't leave them behind to drown," said Alice; "we'll have to take them *and* their containers." And that is what they did.

They next rescued all the working monkeys, the two-headed dog, and the robot cats.

Finally, they made it to the white room, where the water was right up to the necks of the rabbits.

"Oh dear, how you do delay," said a familiar voice.

"But I'm not late," said Alice, as she opened the white boxes that held the rabbits, and lifted them to safety, "and that is what counts."

Alice looked over her bed at the variety of animals sitting on it; there were dogs, cats, mice, guinea pigs, monkeys, rats, rabbits, ferrets and oncomice.

"I wonder what my parents would say if they saw all these animals sitting on my bed," thought Alice. "I don't think they would mind, seeing as what is wrong with them." She then looked at the baby in her arms. "Seeing him now, I don't think he was all baby the last time I looked. I know I thought he was, but seeing him now and seeing how he most definitely looks like a baby now, I would have to say that before he was more dog than a baby."

Alice then returned to the matter in hand. "So where

am I to go now? This was the first room I entered, but I've no idea how I got in here." Just then, Alice noticed the large bolted door that she had tried to open when she was in the room the last time.

"I know – as the water rises I should be able to reach and open the top bolt," thought Alice. "I just hope the bottom one is still open."

The bed floated in circles round the room as the water rose steadily. Alice knew her timing would have to be spot on if she was to open the door. The bed floated past the door; Alice reached out; her fingertips brushed against the bolt.

"Next time, I should be within reach," said Alice; "but if I miss I'm sure by the time I come round again the bolt will be submerged."

She was in position; she reached out and caught it. The bed pulled at her, trying to make her let go, but Alice clung on tight. She then slid the bolt across and pulled at the door.

"It won't budge!" cried Alice in dismay, as she pulled again. "The bottom bolt must be back on!"

"No, nobody has touched it since you opened it," said the White Rabbit. "It must be the weight of the water."

"Oh," sighed Alice despondently, "if only someone would push from the other side, I'm sure we could do it then."

Alice lost her grasp, and sat back, at a loss at what to do next. She noticed the Rabbit staring straight upwards.

"What are you looking at?" Alice asked, looking up. She noticed that one by one the stars were disappearing. Soon all the stars had gone, but this didn't bother the Rabbit as he was staring longingly at the moon.

But the moon was also destined to disappear. And once gone, left the heavens completely black.

The water kept on rising, and seemed to be gaining

more energy. It went straight past the walls of the white room, cascading upwards into the darkness.

"Hold on!" screamed Alice, trying to be heard above the noise of the water.

They went up and up. Alice then noticed a small light. The light got bigger as they approached it at a tremendous speed. Alice could see that the light was coming through a window. Closer still, and Alice could see that on the other side of the window was her bedroom.

"We're getting out!" shrieked Alice joyously.

They got closer and closer until they went through...

...the Square-window.

CHAPTER 13

ALICE'S EVIDENCE

Alice shot out through the television and hit her bed with a jolt. The first thing Alice noticed was that her bedroom was back to normal; there were no trees or plants anywhere, nor animals playing games. She then realised that the water hadn't followed her through the television, nor—

"The animals! The baby!" screamed Alice. She looked about her desperately, but couldn't see them anywhere.

"Oh dear!" cried Alice, "not one of them made it." She then noticed, slowly falling and settling onto her bed, all the photographs.

"At least I still have these," said Alice to herself, "and when I show them to people they are sure to go in there and rescue them."

Alice became quiet as she started to look through the photographs. She saw a picture of the Kitten: the one she had met in the doorway. Alice thought him so sweet. Her eye then caught hold of another picture of a kitten: this one was dead, it had a bolt drilled into its skull, its face—

"Oh no! they are the same kitten!" cried Alice, as she realised what was indeed true. "How could they!" Alice began to cry.

Mary jumped up onto the bed, and sat next to Alice to try to comfort her. Both then started to look through the rest of the photographs. After just a few pictures, Alice looked at Mary and felt she had to say sorry.

They all sat there silently: Alice with her silent

thoughts, Mary with her silent comfort, and the photographs with their silent screams.

* * *

I feel so sad,
From seeing those two pictures of that one cat,
My insides drop,
Leaving my body empty, my mind lost.

It breaks my heart,
I begin to tremble and then tears start,
Feeling sick,
It was in the name of science, they did this.

They look helpless,
The dogs, cats, rabbits, monkeys, just so helpless,
This is wrong,
I feel so ashamed of the human-race,
I have to hold my dog.

* * *

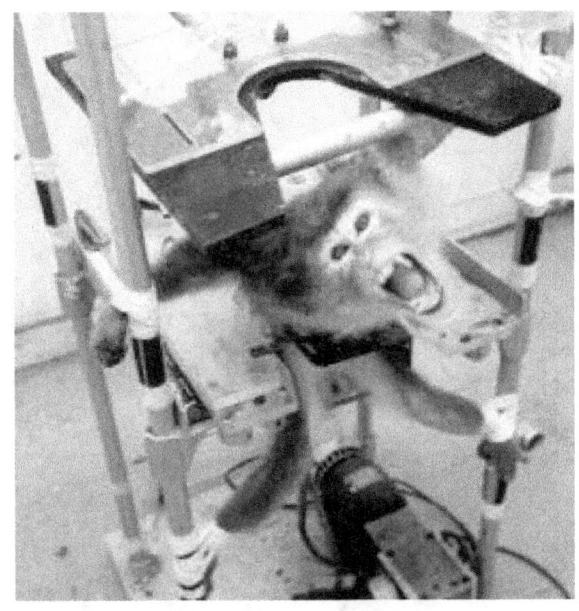

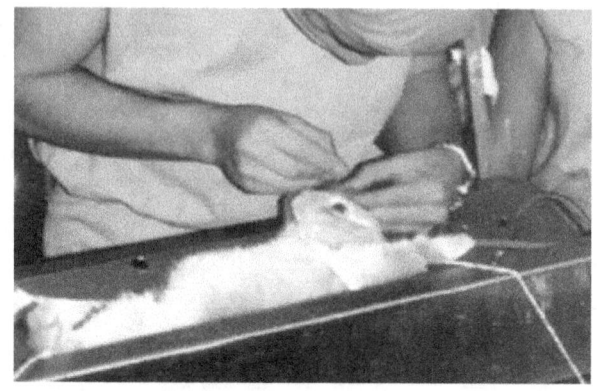

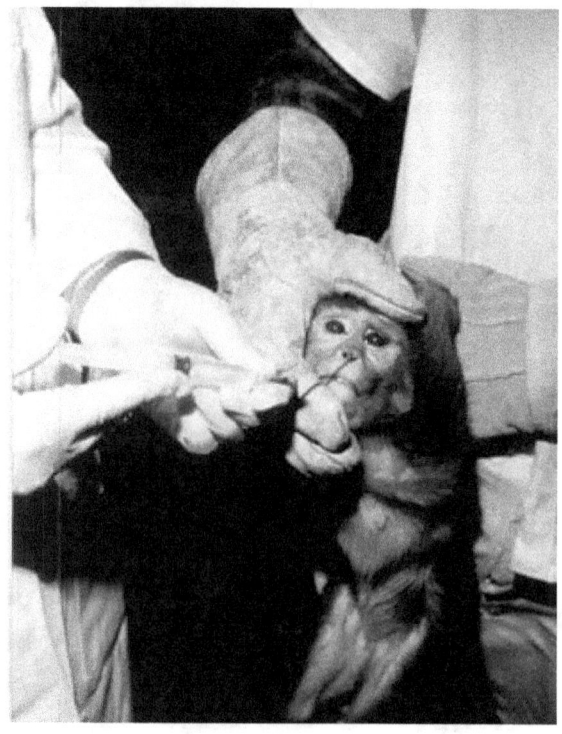

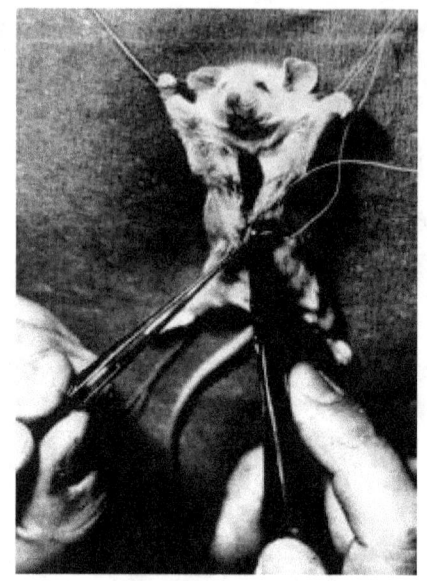

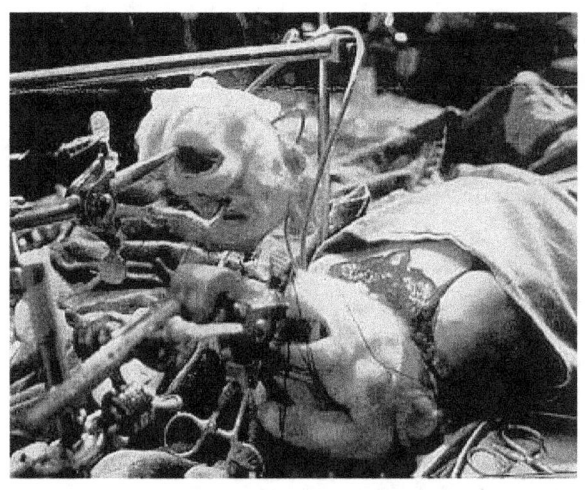

Later that same day, Alice was given her birthday cake. She was asked to blow out the candles then to make a wish. Alice could only look at her family in bewilderment.

They asked her again; after which, Alice stared at the candles. She stared long and hard. She wondered how many more candles the cake needed.

After some more prodding from her family, Alice finally blew out the candles; whereupon, she immediately closed her eyes so she could still see them.

...THE END

I here officially thank you
  for reading this book,
Its content wasn't nice
  but know it we should.

I do have one reservation
  that's with me still,
That Alice was the casualty
  who witnessed this ill.

She was the eternal dreaming child
  but now she's awake,
I can't rectify all that I've done
  only compensate.

Therefore all her sad memories
  I shall here erase,
So she may return to those
  happy summer days.

But your memories dear reader
  shall always remain,
Of the horrific tortures
  they do in your name.

FURTHER READING

Why Animal Experiments Must Stop – and how you can stop them
Vernon Coleman (Green Print, 1991)

The Cruel Deception – the use of animals in medical research
Dr Robert Sharpe (Thorsons, 1988)

Vivisection Or Science – a choice to make
Prof. Pietro Croce, M.D. (Civis, 1991)

ORGANISATIONS

National Anti-Vivisection Society (NAVS)
Millbank Tower, Millbank, London, SW1P 4QP

British Union for the Abolition of Vivisection (BUAV)
16a Crane Grove, London, N7 8NN